WINTER'S SNARE

WINTER BLACK SERIES: SEASON TWO BOOK SIX

MARY STONE

Copyright © 2024 by Mary Stone Publishing

All rights reserved.

No part of this book may be reproduced in any form or by any electronic or mechanical means, including information storage and retrieval systems, without written permission from the author, except for the use of brief quotations in a book review.

❦ Created with Vellum

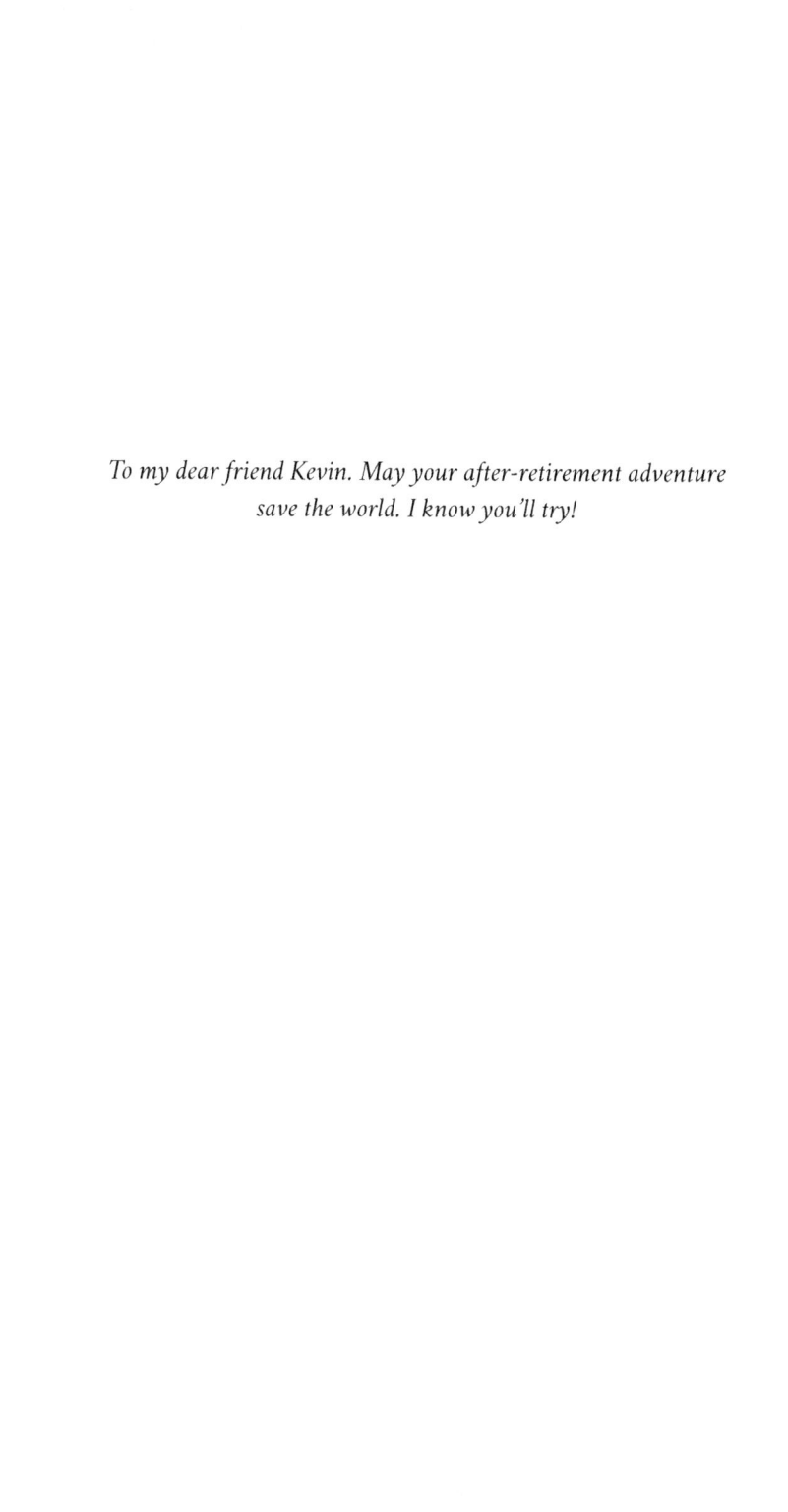

To my dear friend Kevin. May your after-retirement adventure save the world. I know you'll try!

DESCRIPTION

Love is the beginning of everything. And the end.

Haunted by dreams of the boy whose life she shattered and burdened by dark family secrets she's only just begun to understand, Private Investigator Winter Black is trying to keep her life from falling apart. With her husband on a yearlong break from the FBI, the bills are piling up, and Winter has no choice but to take on even the most mundane cases. Serving a summons should be easy.

Until the man she served is found dead the next day. His wife too.

The man, a local appliance store owner, faced financial ruin pending the legal case, leading authorities to suspect a murder-suicide. Winter doesn't buy that he killed himself or his wife. In fact, she'd seen the anticipation in his eyes as they packed for a vacation together—hardly the behavior of a man about to end it all. When the employee behind the lawsuit goes missing, Winter is convinced.

Someone murdered the couple. But who?

As she digs deeper, the bodies start to pile up. People

connected to the case are being picked off one by one, and Winter can't shake the feeling that she's getting closer to something dangerous—something that wants to stay hidden. Someone's playing a twisted game, and Winter's caught right in the middle.

With a target on her back.

The mystery and suspense continue with Winter's Snare, the heart-stopping sixth book in the Winter Black Season Two series. It's a reminder that love endures all things. Except murder.

1

Nick Riley blinked into the hazy darkness and groaned as his head throbbed with a deep, pulsing ache. He could barely make out the ceiling above him—a patchy grid of water-stained tiles, the scent of old smoke hanging heavy in the air.

Where the hell am I?

His mind fumbled through a fog of confusion, trying to piece together how he'd gotten to this place. He shifted slightly, grimacing at the scratchy burn of dirty carpet beneath his cheek. The pain in his head sharpened as he moved, and he lifted a hand to his cheek.

That was when he noticed the blood—warm and sticky, matting his hair and streaking his face. Where it oozed from his ear stung with every pulse of his heartbeat.

Someone had jumped into his car. The memory struck him like a sudden jolt.

He'd been stopped at a back road intersection on his way home, barely paying attention, when the door had opened and someone—no, some*thing*—had lunged into his passenger seat. He barely had time to register the figure, let alone react, before a blunt force struck the side of his head.

Nick could see the small metal truncheon now, tight in his attacker's hairy hand. God, it had hurt. His stomach turned as he recalled the moment he blacked out, the brief, disorienting sensation of being dragged from his car like dead weight.

Now he was in a second location. And every idiot who ever watched a crime show knew what that meant—certain death was next. So why, Nick wondered, was he still alive?

He had no idea who the hell the guy was or why the man attacked him in the first place, but that was of little concern at the moment.

Nick forced himself to focus. The room seemed eerily familiar, though Nick had never been there before. He was sure of that. But it reminded him of a skeezy place he'd once gone to buy weed. A sticky sheen of old cigarette smoke clung to the unadorned walls, plaster flaking in places where it had been struck with fists and whatever else. The beige, builder-grade carpet was black in places. Stained with bong water or burns or whatever else no one bothered to clean up.

The man had dropped him, unconscious, on that filthy carpet. Must've thought he'd stay that way, because now the guy was talking on the phone, his back turned.

Nick had to do something now. It was his only chance.

He drew himself up slowly. The boards under the carpet creaked, and Nick's head spun. He'd never had such a headache. He wasn't even sure he could run, but he didn't have a choice.

Run or die. Those were his options.

He was in a living room, and just beyond the open doorway, he heard the faint buzz of a refrigerator. Nick kept his gaze on the man as he edged toward the noise. Then he saw it. Around a sidewall, where he assumed a hallway would be, was a back door with a greasy curtain hanging haphazardly to one side of a small window. Outside, the sky was dark.

Nick's gaze darted back to the man. He was tall and skinny. A greenish tattoo curled around his forearm—a prison tat. Over his hair, he wore a bandanna, a shade of red now so faded it looked pink.

Nick couldn't understand what the man was saying. His voice was rough and thick, mumbling like Eddie Vedder. Did he think Nick was dead? The man wasn't even wearing a mask or any kind of disguise. But a quick pulse check would've verified otherwise.

It didn't matter. Nick wasn't dead, but he would be soon if he didn't escape this room. He swallowed hard and crept toward the back door.

His hand trembled as he reached for the knob. It turned, but when he pulled, the door didn't move. A faint clunk sounded, and panic ripped up his spine. Nick flinched and looked over his shoulder.

The man hadn't noticed.

With a deep swallow, Nick turned back around and studied the door. The dead bolt was locked. Nick braced himself, turned the thumb lock, and threw the door open. He began to run.

"Hey!" The man's voice roared like a lion behind him.

Nick cried out and galloped down several crumbling concrete stairs into an overgrown yard. Barefoot and wobbly, he raced through thistle and milkweed. The property was enclosed by a six-foot wooden fence patched with chicken wire, but Nick spotted where a fallen tree branch had knocked a section down. He could scramble over that and run to the nearest house. It looked far away, across an abandoned field, but he reckoned it was possible. Just barely.

He put everything he had into sprinting the distance.

As he bounded over a pile of old leaves, the ground dropped out from under him. One foot slipped into empty space, his other catching on the edge of the hole. A hideous crack echoed through Nick's whole body as he plummeted into darkness.

He flailed helplessly in the narrow shaft, arms and legs ricocheting off the rough brick walls as he tumbled deeper. His head smacked the side with a dull thud, sending sparks across his vision.

He splashed into a waist-high pool of water with a sickening crash, landing hard on his side and back. Icy water soaked through his clothes as he broke the surface, gasping for air, his body twisted and aching from the fall.

Pain erupted in his leg as he struggled to sit up, the sharp edge of bone jutting through his skin. Tears filled his eyes, the agony almost blinding. A warm trickle of blood ran down the back of his neck where his head had struck the wall, but the cold water and adrenaline kept him alert.

He should've been blinded by all the pain, but the rush of animalistic panic muffled it. He had to get out of there, away from the man.

Nick touched the slimy stone walls all around him—a square opening no more than two feet across. He looked up and saw the moon. Or part of it anyway. Something was blocking his view.

The silhouette of a man's head, staring down.

"Help!" Nick clawed at the walls, trying to climb up, but he was fifteen feet or more underground. Trapped.

Stars glittered beyond the man's shoulders, his face concealed in shadow.

"Why are you doing this to me?" Nick tasted blood now. Blood and bile and something rotten in the water. The smell hit him next.

Gagging, he realized chunks of something were floating

all around him, bumping into him, sticking to his exposed skin. Without thinking, Nick grabbed one—something long and skinny, shaped vaguely like a serving spoon. He lifted it to the moonlight.

Bone. A bone with rotting meat still clinging to it.

Too horrified to even scream, Nick dropped it. A sickly splash of the filthy water shot up and slapped him on the cheek. "Let me out! Let me out!"

Without a word, the man disappeared. Nick was granted one final look at the shimmering night sky before the well cover slammed shut on screaming metal hinges, shrouding him in blackness.

The inky dark around him pressed in, sharp, spiky waves of pain pulsing through his broken leg before breaking like fireworks over his whole body. "Come back! Please. Help! Help! Help!"

He screamed until the echo of his own voice was intolerable. Then he covered his ears with both hands and screamed more.

"Somebody! Help me!"

Water sloshed against him as high as his chest, caressing him with lumps of bone and flesh. The stink and taste of the place on his lips was unbearable. He grabbed at the walls again and again, but there was nothing to hold on to. And even if his fingers could find purchase, he couldn't climb a sheer vertical cylinder with a bone poking through one leg.

Despair wrapped him like a blanket soaked in tar. His limbs grew heavy as his heart began to slow. The pain from his leg filtered in bit by bit, growing in intensity until there was nothing left for him to do but cry. His voice echoed up the shaft and boomeranged back down for added torture.

With every hissing breath, waves danced across the puddle, causing those fleshy bones to poke at him, sickening him to his core. He tried to hold it back, but vomit filled his throat and spackled his windpipe. He leaned to the side and let it out into the stinking liquid. He choked and heaved, the smell of the place making him vomit more and more until there was nothing left but dry gasps.

Nick found himself vaguely hoping the wound in his leg had torn a hole in his femoral artery so he could bleed out quickly. Or maybe the head wound would do it. If he was going to die in this putrid darkness, he wanted to die fast. Go numb and fade into the nothingness so he could fly away from it all.

He thought about how no one would even know where he was. No one was coming. Not now, not ever. He would just rot down here, his body dissolving and mingling with all the others in this nightmare soup.

Would anyone care that he was missing? Would there even be headlines about his mysterious disappearance, the fruitless searches, his friends and family waiting for a closure that would never come? Would anyone even care?

Yes. His mom.

She'd never stop looking for him. She'd never stop waiting for him to walk through the door. Even if they told her to give up hope, she wouldn't. Never.

Nick could picture her sitting by the window, watching for him like she used to when he was a kid—waiting for him to come home safe after riding his skateboard around the neighborhood. She'd be the only one who cared enough to keep searching, to believe he was still out there somewhere.

That thought hurt more than the shattered bone jutting through his skin. He hated the idea of leaving her with nothing but questions, with an empty chair at the holidays, and the burden of wondering for the rest of her life what had happened to her son.

His throat was so dry, and his mouth tasted vile. He smacked his lips, longing for water. Just a few more sips before the darkness swallowed him whole. But there was nothing he could drink. Only the cold, the stink, and the agony that rippled through his body with every shallow breath.

To distract himself from the endless suffering, he tried to hold on to a memory of his mom—her smile, her laugh—but the pain made everything slippery, impossible to grasp. Time crept on, his mind growing fuzzier, his thoughts more abstract, until a sort of merciful sleep took over.

Nick's last thought before falling unconscious was a prayer to never wake up. It would be easier that way—for both of them. Just slip into the void and leave the pain, the cold, the terror behind. No more waiting. No more wondering. Just peace.

Finally.

2

Winter Black stood alone on the road, a cold wind lifting her hair and nipping at her flesh. She couldn't see the end in either direction, just an endless twisting of black asphalt. Like a snake with no tail slithering through gray clouds...

Choosing a direction at random, she took a step, then another. If she ran fast enough and long enough, maybe she could find the end of it. She needed to know where this road was heading or what it was taking her away from. Far in the distance, at the very edge of her vision, she thought she saw the red glow—her trustworthy beacon.

Faster and faster, her feet barely striking the pavement, she ran. A shrill scream cut into the padded rhythm of her running. It felt like a knife to the gut, arresting her body in an instant. Another scream rang out, and then a shot, followed by the crack of a bone. Distant laughter echoed back to her, like the rumble of thunder on a quiet plain.

Winter turned on her heel. In the middle of the road was a deep sinkhole. A tiny hand reached out from it, pale as the moon on a winter's night.

She raced closer, peered down, and got a look at the person's face—wide brown eyes, messy golden-brown hair, soft and innocent features.

Timothy Stewart. The boy whose life she had destroyed in an instant. The boy who would never forgive her.

"Grab my hand!" She reached for him again and again, but the harder she tried, the farther away his hand seemed to be. The ground rumbled and pulled him in deeper, a hellmouth eating its prey.

"No!" Winter got flat on her stomach and reached into the pit but gasped at what she saw under him. Fire and corpses with decaying arms pulling the boy down.

"Grab my hand!" Winter was leaning halfway into the pit now. "Tim, please! Let me help you!"

The monsters sank their claws in. Winter fumbled to grab him, screaming as he tumbled into the blackness.

Winter awoke in a cold sweat, her head swimming. She sat up in bed, laboring for breath. For a moment, everything was blurry, so she could see nothing but the inhuman zombie faces of the monsters dragging Timothy Stewart down into hell with them.

"Winter?" Her husband's hand fell gently on her back—warm and comforting. Her breath was shaky, freezing and hot all at once. "It's okay, darlin'. You're safe. Everything's all right. You were dreaming."

She tried to speak, but her bottom lip quivered, and she sucked in a painful gasp. Slowly, the details of the bedroom came into focus. Sunlight peeked through the little gap in the curtains. She rubbed her palm over her forehead, feeling the pulse of her heartbeat in her aching temples.

"I'm okay." She forced a smile as weak as it was fake. "I'm fine."

"Tell me what you dreamed about?"

Turning to face Noah, Winter finally managed to inhale a full breath. The slant of sunlight cut right across his face so she could make out the green of his eyes, soft and gentle. Wanting nothing more than to help her.

She'd suffered from nightmares most of her life. Only since marrying Noah had there been someone to help her through them. Sighing, she fell into his strong arms and borrowed his strength until she was able to regather her own.

"Was it about Opal?" As Noah said the name of her biological aunt, she cringed a little. Winter had never even met the woman, having made her acquaintance on the phone for the first time in the previous week.

Two phone conversations. That was the extent of their relationship before Winter learned the woman was dead. Found dead in her car.

Between that and the memory of the strange text she'd received, Winter hadn't really processed the whole thing yet.

Every family has its secrets. But you can't keep secrets from me.

She wasn't sure what to think about it, and the only thoughts she did have were too horrible to let stand.

She shook her head against her husband's chest, relishing the soft feel of his cotton t-shirt and the scent of his skin. This was her home more than any place had ever been or could be.

"Tim," she whispered, his name sour on her tongue. Saying it out loud was like a shot of vinegar to the back of her throat.

"Again?" Noah tried to suppress his sigh but failed. He squeezed her tighter.

"It was different this time. He was being sucked down into hell, and I was trying to help him. But he wouldn't let me. The closer I got, the deeper he fell."

Noah rubbed one heavy hand over her shoulders and used the other to brush back strands of sweaty black hair that had fallen onto her face. "Was this a dream or was it a *dream?*"

Winter knew exactly what he was asking—if she was just dreaming like everybody else did or if this was one of her visions. She wished she could give him a clear answer, but the truth was, she often didn't know the difference until reality came to bear out the story.

"Maybe I should go check on him. I still have his uncle's address."

"We could do that." The exhaustion in Noah's voice was unmistakable. She knew the last thing her husband wanted was to be around the little boy who'd buried a knife in his guts in a wild effort to protect Justin, the man who'd tortured him for months.

Winter shook her head against Noah's chest. "The closer I get, the worse off he is."

"What happened to Tim is not your fault." Noah touched her chin, lifting her face to look into her eyes. "And what happens to him from here on out is not your responsibility."

She nodded, because she knew that, logically, he was right, even if she didn't really believe it.

Pulling away from her husband's touch, Winter swung her legs over the side of the bed. Her toes squished into the soft faux sheepskin rug on the floor. She pushed to her feet and headed toward the bathroom.

"You can't fix the past." Noah watched her from his place in the bed. "Tim is safe now. He's with his family. You've done everything you can for him. It's time to let him go."

She paused, a hand on the doorframe, and looked back over her shoulder. "Don't you understand that I can't?"

He didn't answer. Silence pooled between them like brackish water until she couldn't stand it a moment longer. She slipped into the bathroom and closed the door, pressing her back against it. The memory of that day—the day Justin forced her to betray a little boy and ruin his entire life—was fighting to overtake her.

She pressed a hand to her chest and closed her eyes. "Breathe." A tear sprang to her cheek, stinging her skin. "Just breathe."

Winter got to work earlier than usual. Noah had to go into the office one last time to clean out his things and put everything in order before his year-long sabbatical officially began. She was excited that he was going to be around more often. They'd have more time to spend together as a couple, and he'd be there to help her with her cases should she need him.

Not to mention, he'd finally have time to build that brick barbecue he'd been going on about since they bought the dang house. More than that, she was happy Noah would get a break. It was clear how much the job had been wearing on him since they'd relocated from Richmond to Austin.

She was almost jealous. Almost. The truth was, Winter wasn't sure what she would do with herself if she wasn't working.

Go rock climbing, she thought with a smirk. Her last case had led her straight to her new favorite hobby, and she was anxious to truly get started with it. Maybe Noah would like to go climbing with her again. She couldn't remember the last time she'd had more fun with him than when they were rappelling down that cliff in the wildlife reserve.

Granted, they'd been on their way to a crime scene, but she was pretty sure climbing would be just as much fun without a dead body at the end of their rope.

She'd ordered a bunch of gear for them online. The package would be coming in the next few days.

Taking a sip of her mocha latte, Winter sat down at her desk and pressed the power button on her computer. Usually by the time she got in, her assistant, Ariel Joyner, was already at her desk tapping away at her pastel pink keyboard. She'd almost gotten used to having Kline there too—her recently unearthed biological father who she'd employed as a makeshift contractor to give her little office a serious facelift.

The place was bright and shiny on the outside—all clean glass and green trim, but the truth was the bones were a bit shaky. So far, Kline had ripped up the old shop carpet and sanded and sealed the hardwood underneath, installed new carpet, painted the walls, added new molding, and built her new, beautiful shelving. Now nobody could mistake her business for anything other than a well-oiled, moneymaking machine.

Still, though, the bathrooms still left a little something to be desired. Kline had resolved to work on them next. The faucet leaked, the ceiling tiles were brown from old water stains, and there was a smell. It wasn't strong—in fact, it was so faint that the smell faded after a while—but there was the vaguest whiff of sewer. Kline said it was because the wax seal on the toilet needed to be replaced.

But, recovered from his kidnapping scare, Kline had disappeared like a thief in the night to go visit his sister.

Unfortunately, Opal had been murdered in her car two mornings back and was now lying on a table in a morgue somewhere. And Kline, who the authorities found in her home, was being retained for questioning.

For a moment, the office disappeared around Winter as she asked herself whether she believed Kline had something to do with Opal's death. And the answer was that she truly didn't know.

Best not to think too much about it, Winter decided. She took another sip of her latte. What she needed to think about now was finding new cases and new clients. After all, with Noah taking a sabbatical at one-third his usual salary, Winter was going to have to pick up the slack. It was her turn, after all. He'd helped finance her business, keeping Black Investigations afloat while she was in the red. Now she had to return the favor.

As Winter scrolled through the dull initial intake forms to decide which cases she should pick up, her thoughts wandered back to her nightmare. Back to Timothy Stewart and the bony hands dragging him down.

Maybe Noah was right, and she needed to let him go. He was safe now. Justin would spend the rest of his life in prison so he could no longer hurt Tim or anybody else.

Just let it go.

But how could she when the boy's misery was her fault? How could she just forget about him, knowing the scars of what Justin had done to him would never heal? She knew, because she carried the exact same scars—scabbed-over wounds that opened at will and pulsed blood and black bile all over her life.

Again, Winter thought about driving over to visit Tim. Just to make sure he was settling in okay. It was her dream that warned her back. The more she fought to reach him, the deeper he sank.

Maybe the dream was a vision, and the vision was warning her to stay away.

The bell over the door dinged, and Winter flinched. Her office had once been a shoe store, so the whole front-facing wall was a fishbowl. It let her see who was coming before they walked inside. The heads-up eased her ever-present paranoia. But sometimes, like now, she would get distracted, and someone would sneak up on her. Luckily, it was just Ariel arriving at eight sharp, like she did every morning.

"Hey, Winter." Ariel smiled brightly. Twenty-four years

old with a round face and bouncy brown curls, she was dressed in jeans and a silk floral blouse.

Winter still wore pretty much what she had when she was an FBI agent—navy blue slacks and a button-down. Why bother getting a new wardrobe? In fact, dressing like an agent helped her blend in at crime scenes, move comfortably through rank, and keep her sidearm concealed whenever she chose to carry one.

She'd been hoping to break the habit of always carrying a gun when she moved into the private sector, but that was starting to feel like wishful thinking.

"Good morning." Winter forced a friendly smile. She glanced at the summons sitting on her desk and considered asking Ariel to deliver it to its final destination. Her fingers and her voice hesitated. Tasks like this would give her eager young assistant a taste of what the job was really like day-to-day—not just shootouts and undercover operations, but a lot of boring menial work.

Then again, a drive might give Winter a chance to clear her head.

"Could you go through the intake forms and pick up some new cases for us?" Winter rose from her desk, the summons envelope in her grip.

"You want me to?" Ariel blinked, her brown eyes big. "I guess I can. Do you have any criteria?"

"Whichever pays the most and requires the least effort."

If I was smart, that would always be the criteria.

"You got it, Boss." Ariel nodded and settled behind her desk as Winter moved toward the door.

The summons wasn't going to deliver itself.

3

Winter parked on the street and studied the nice neighborhood for a minute. Pleasant environment or not, she was serving someone, so she opened her glove box, grabbed her new .38 Special Revolver, and secured it in an ankle strap around her left leg before snatching up the summons papers.

After double-checking that she had the right address, she stepped out of her Honda Pilot onto the narrow road. A few houses down, she noticed a man in his backyard using an edger, the buzz filling up the atmosphere. She didn't see anybody else around.

The house was lovely and well-maintained, a two-story craftsman with dahlias growing out front and a chef's herb garden near the front bay window. In the driveway was a huge RV, all shiny chrome and fresh paint. The door to the bay underneath was open, and it looked like somebody was either loading or unloading for a trip.

She walked up the path and passed a *For Sale* sign with a smiling picture of a real estate agent on it. As she stepped past a couple of garden gnomes and onto the porch, she heard a bump in the RV behind her and faint notes of "dad rock" playing inside. Winter withdrew her finger from the doorbell and approached the RV.

"Hello?"

A few bumps emanated from inside, and then a moment later, a man stepped out. With balding hair, a deep scowl, and a big, round belly, he looked like thirty-five going on sixty. He had a wide nose and a mole just to the left of a furled nostril, and he stood a little shorter than her own five-seven. There was something familiar about him, though she couldn't quite place it. Something that brought to mind washers and dryers.

Weird. She shook her head at herself.

"What do you want?" He walked to the pile of stuff sitting in the driveway.

Winter glanced down and noticed a few grocery bags filled with food and soda. The smell about him was familiar too—woody and sweet. Bourbon.

"Are you Brent Ballstow?" Winter asked.

"That's me. What can I do you for?"

She held out the envelope, and he quickly snatched it from her fingers. He ripped it open—though there was no need. All he had to do was push in the little metal tab. As he read the summons, his face began to flush with anger.

"You've been served." Her tone was neutral.

"Who the hell do you think you are, coming to my private home to give me this horseshit!" Ballstow tossed the papers back in her face. The wind caught them, and they fluttered here and there, none of them coming anywhere near her, though.

"I'm just the messenger."

"You're a fucking scumbag, that's what you are!" Ballstow stomped toward her, and Winter's entire body stiffened. The look in his eyes was wild, his lips twisting with grimaces and snarls. "This whole thing's a damn joke. You hear me? I'm not gonna play this time. I am not going to play!"

"Brent?" A woman peeked her head out the front door and peered down the drive toward the RV. She had dark hair perfectly styled in a short bob like an old-timey flapper girl, and she was wearing so much makeup, Winter could make out her blue-and-purple eyeshadow from across the lawn. "Everything okay?"

"Go inside, Lily." The man shook his head like a bulldog. "I got it handled."

The woman did not obey but rather stepped out onto the porch and even took a few tentative steps closer.

"If you've got a problem, you'll have to take it up with the court. Have a nice day." Winter shrugged and put on her sunglasses. There was no reason for her to get involved, no reason for her continued presence. She turned on her heel to head toward her SUV.

"Don't you walk away from me. I'm not finished with you yet!" Ballstow lunged and latched onto Winter's arm, whipping her around. Before she could stop herself, she snatched the man by his shirt, slammed his body hard into the side of the RV, and twisted his arm up behind him.

"Don't ever touch me."

"Get off me!" His whimpers were pathetic under her tight grip. She knew damn well it hurt.

Winter let go, and he nearly fell to his knees before catching himself. She took a step back, righted her jacket, and popped her neck.

As Winter walked back to her Honda, Lily rushed down from the porch and ran to his side. In the reflection of her own passenger window, Winter watched the woman, presumably his wife, hold his shoulders. Checking him over for injuries as if he were a beloved child.

"I'm fine. It's fine." He rubbed the back of his neck with an open palm. "It's just Nick. Doing what he said he would do, despite my warning him not to."

"Why, that dirty little…" Lily clenched her tiny fist. "We'll get him in court. He doesn't have a case, and he knows it."

Winter got into the driver's seat and fired up her engine. When she glanced back at the couple, they were hugging. The man's hand was in his wife's hair, petting it gently, and her eyes were closed. Despite the circumstances, there was something incredibly pure about the scene. Something that almost compelled Winter to forgive the heathen for putting his hands on her.

Winter realized that feeling was just her missing her own husband. His hands in her hair, her head on his shoulder. With everything that had been happening lately—from family drama to high-profile homicides—they hadn't had a lot of time to just be together as a couple lately. Though she still slept next to him every single night, that didn't stop her from missing him like crazy during the day.

Part of her wanted to give Brent Ballstow the benefit of the doubt, reasoning that he'd simply lost his cool and maybe wasn't such a bad guy after all. Part of her was angry at herself for not dislocating his shoulder. He'd have bruises on his arm in the shape of her fingerprints, though. Hopefully, that would be enough to teach him to keep his hands to himself.

And the last part of her was really glad she'd purchased another gun since dealing with the latest crop of criminals—spies, kidnappers, and heartbroken serial killers.

She put the gun back in her glove box. She hadn't needed it, but the cold steel against her leg had given her a genuine sense of security.

4

Noah slapped a scribbled sticky note on a manila folder that he added to the catawampus pile on his desk. He'd never been what might be called fastidious with filing, so even though he'd only worked at the Bureau in Austin for a few months, he had a huge mess to clean up before he could officially begin his sabbatical.

"I think you're probably the biggest butthead I've ever known." Eve's feet were up on her desk, rollie chair leaned far back so her long yellow ponytail swung freely. "And I will never, ever forgive you for this."

Noah tried not to snort. It wasn't the first time she'd said that. He had a feeling it wouldn't be the last.

"I'm sorry." He yanked another file from his desk drawer and opened it to examine the contents.

"Don't lie to me, you giant turd."

Laughing, he scrawled another label on a sticky note. Last time he was in this tiny, cramped, windowless office, he'd felt like the walls were closing in as the oxygen was being sucked out. Now it was just another room.

He could even conjure some affection for the place now

that he was leaving its confines. How different a prison felt to the guard versus the convict or an asylum felt for the visitor versus the patient. He was free to go whenever he liked, and that made everything better.

"That's the last of them." Noah slapped the desk drawer closed. "I can email you everything else, and you can always call me if you need anything."

"Traitor." Eve turned her nose up at him. "Tell me you're at least going to do something fun while you're off. Take that wife of yours somewhere nice."

"Somewhere nice…" He rubbed his chin in thought. "Like Applebee's?"

Eve coughed out a laugh. "I was thinking more like the Bahamas."

"But vets eat free once a year. Twice if you include dessert for my birthday." He threw her a big shit-eating grin.

A light tap on the open door drew their attention.

A second later, SSA Weston Falkner stepped inside with the grace and precision of a well-oiled robot. He was dressed in his gray suit as always, his white hair slicked back and his stony face clean-shaven. Still, there was something friendlier about his expression today. Not a smile per se…more like his scowl wasn't quite as deep.

"Good morning. Looks like you're nearly finished getting everything in order?"

"Yes, sir." Noah nodded. Reaching down, he picked up the cardboard box filled with his personal items and moved it to the desk. "I was just about to head out."

"I'm glad I caught you. There's been a development in one of your old cases. I thought you might be interested."

Noah lifted his eyebrows. "What's up?"

Falkner smoothed his tie. "I assume you two remember Grace Schumaker?"

"How could I forget?" Eve groaned as if in pain.

Though Noah didn't make any noise, he absolutely sympathized. The Schumaker case was probably the most personally affecting case he'd had to deal with since joining the Austin VCU.

Grace was a teenager, the daughter of a man who sexually abused her when she was very young before casting her aside when she got too old to retain his interest. As a way of getting revenge on him and on the world, she'd become deeply involved in a human-trafficking ring—kidnapping young women and then selling them to the highest bidder.

Noah would never forget the scene where the kidnapped girls were being held—beaten, drugged, sleeping on top of one another in cramped, filthy quarters. Many of them were immigrants or minorities, people who were easier to hurt because they were invisible to so much of society. And some of them were young enough to be in elementary school.

It also happened to be the first case he and Eve had worked together.

"Parts of the ring are still operational. If we don't shut it down completely, there's no reason why they wouldn't start ramping back up. We have a lead from our guy in the field that an exchange will be taking place this Thursday at a gas station in Lytle." Falkner dropped a folder on Noah's desk. "Interested?"

Noah cracked open the folder and flicked through the contents. Once again—trapped in a room with the fearsome gargoyle who'd been making his life hell ever since he came back to Texas—a familiar hand twisted Noah's guts. "I thought you wanted me out?"

"It's not personal." Falkner shrugged and perched his butt on the edge of Eve's desk. "You've been distracted, and that's dangerous in our line of work. Tell me I'm wrong."

Noah folded his lips in and cocked his head.

Unexpectedly, a chuckle broke through. "Dammit. You're not wrong."

To Noah's astonishment, Falkner cracked a smile. "I've taken two sabbaticals in my career. There's no shame in it. This job'll put you in the grave if you let it. It's my sincere hope that, when the year's through, you'll come back and put your nose back to the old grindstone. I'll be retired by then, of course. You'll have someone brand new to annoy."

That made Noah a little sad. He couldn't be sure why. "So that's what this is about? Get me out of the office long enough that I become someone else's problem?"

Falkner put his hands up in surrender. "You caught me."

Noah smiled in disbelief. His gaze drifted to Eve, who had a very *I told you so* kind of expression on her face.

Where the hell had this guy been the last few months? He wasn't so bad, this guy. Noah could've put up with him.

"I know this case was personal to you." Falkner tapped the folder with the tip of his long, pale finger. "And while it's never a good idea to get emotionally involved in a case, it's hard to keep your distance when kids are involved. There are cases I'd come back from the grave to work on if given the chance."

Noah nodded, knowing exactly how that felt. "I think you're right. This is a loose end I would like to tie up personally."

Falkner drew himself back to his feet. "It goes without saying that you do everything in your power to be certain I don't regret giving you this opportunity."

"Yes, sir."

Falkner narrowed his gaze, giving Noah a final once-over. Then he drifted out of the office without another word.

Eve pushed off the wall with one foot and rolled her chair to the edge of his desk. "I told you he wasn't the devil."

Noah jabbed his finger at her. "I knew you were about to say that."

"You're still a traitor." She snatched the file from his desk and propped it open on her lap. "But I guess I'm willing to forgive you."

"Thank you." He forced himself not to smile too warmly. He didn't want her to know just how worried he'd been about her being genuinely angry at him. He really liked Eve. She'd done everything to try to make him feel welcome here, and he was going to miss her. "Maybe when I come back, we could team up again?"

Eve's gaze remained on the file, but her mischievous spark dimmed a touch. "Whaddaya say, jarhead? Ready for one last rodeo before we put you out to pasture?"

Noah laughed in spite of himself. "Try and stop me."

5

The week before all this started, my sons and I had just come back from a hunting trip where I bagged a fat white-tail doe. After Troy cleaned the carcass, I had him toss the bones and useless skin and viscera down that old, dried-up well out back. I'd never understood how he forgot to close the lid. It stank like the devil's own ass crack, the smell reaching across the yard.

Troy was rotting his brains out with drugs—that had to be it. I ought to do something about that boy. But that was another worry for another day. Right now, I was worried about Nick Riley. Thanks to my son's ineptitude, my hostage had taken a serious fall and probably broke some bones. With all the dead things down there, sickness could leak right through the skin. I could hardly think of anything worse.

When I saw Nick trip and fall, my first thought was to try to fish him out. I'd have to bring my truck around and hook up the winch, work with him to get him to grab ahold of something. The way he was screaming, I thought some of his bones were probably broken—in which case, I might've actually had to go down the well to grab him myself.

I would've done it for either of my idiot sons, but for this moron, who I didn't know from Adam...

His screams of agony landed like blaring trumpets on my ears, though. And the way he begged and pleaded and cried after he fell...I couldn't stand it. Even though this place was in the country on a couple of acres, I worried someone might hear. So I closed the lid, locking him in the darkness.

I was nervous to tell the boss about this, though, because the plan was to scare Nick, not injure him. Or worse.

She laughed when I admitted what had happened, like I'd made a really funny joke. She always said I was terrible at making jokes because I was too stupid to come up with a punch line that everybody didn't already expect. But I came up with a good one this time. Well, Nick did.

Why did the man fall down the well? Because he couldn't see that well.

The boss said that Nick being dead actually made the next step in her plan better. She just assumed he was dead, and I went along with it because she was so delighted with me. I didn't know what "the next step in the plan" was, but I trusted it. She hadn't let me in on the whole plan for fear I might screw things up. But I'd do anything she asked, no matter how foul or disgusting.

After talking with her, I thought about going out back and finishing Nick off. But why bother? I didn't want to smell it, and I didn't want to hear him—with his pathetic, desperate begging.

What difference did it really make? Nobody could survive down there anyway. If he hadn't run in the first place, he wouldn't be down there. It was his own damn fault.

But that had been three days ago—and he was still alive. All day he'd be quiet, but when it grew late, as I lay in bed, I could hear him. Faint at first, like the whir of a vacuum cleaner. But the quieter my surroundings got, the louder the sound grew from the well. I thought about sleeping at my place in town, but the boys were here, and we worked as a team, so I needed to stay in the country.

"Come back!" his reedy voice screamed. "Help me! Please!"

I turned on my swamp cooler last night to cover the noise so the boys wouldn't hear. They were already deep enough in this operation because of me. They didn't need to be listening to that. And what if Miss Rosemary heard? Her house was two acres over, and her ears weren't what they used to be, but still.

Again, I thought I ought to open the hatch and finish him off, but the memory of the smell stopped me. The boss was happy, and time would take care of Nick. Sooner or later, the screaming would stop, and everything would work itself out. Just like the boss had promised.

For now, it was time to move on to the next part of the plan, which took place far away from Nick and his eerie cries for help.

Wanting to give the loving couple a chance to settle down for the night, I'd been sitting in my truck outside their house for the last three hours, until the clock hit midnight.

When I first arrived, they'd been about to get into their RV to go camping for a long weekend. I couldn't let them skip town. RV parks were not ideal places to be murdering people, since they'd likely be parked right alongside another family. Too many opportunities for witnesses.

I wanted to kill him with my own gun—it had a suppressor—but the boss said I had to use Brent's 9mm.

Otherwise, the kill wouldn't look natural. She was right, as usual.

The RV had only one spare tire. So when they both went inside to grab a few more things, I ran over and let the air out of two of the tires with a Phillips screwdriver. They'd have to get the thing into the shop. No travel for them.

Brent and Lily seemed appropriately irked when they came out to leave and noticed the problem. They talked about it, standing outside staring at the tires, wondering what might've happened. Eventually, they unloaded the groceries they'd packed in the RV and drank a couple of beers on their front porch, holding hands and staring at the stars.

That was hard to watch, the hand-holding part. They'd been together for so long—over a decade at this point—and they were still holding hands. I couldn't remember the last time…

Never mind. I needed to focus on the job in front of me. Get it done. Then get on the horn to the boss and let her know the mission was accomplished. With Lily and Brent out of the way—and now Nick—she'd feel safe again, and we could start our life together, just like I'd been dreaming about.

I pulled out the key my boss had given me for the job and made my way around to the back of the house. There was a dead bolt on the door, but the same key that opened the knob opened that up too.

What the hell extra security was that?

As I turned the knob and eased the door open, I heard the faint sound of a television. Somebody might still be awake. Panic surged through me. I took a minute to steel myself. The job had to be done tonight. I couldn't mess this up. I couldn't get distracted.

Placing one foot right in front of the other like I did when tracking a deer, I stalked into the house.

I very carefully inched open the first drawer closest to the back door in the kitchen, and there it was. Brent's gun was just sitting there waiting for me, just as my instructions promised.

Not the brightest place to keep a gun, but I'd seen worse. I mean, the boys propped a rifle by the front door even though I kept warning against that.

When I slid the magazine out, all the rounds were there. More than enough for tonight's work.

Peering out from the kitchen into the living room, I saw the back of Brent's head from behind where he sat on the couch watching TV. A true crime documentary about Gary Ridgway, aka the Green River Killer.

I wasn't sure if that was funny or sad. I guessed if I ended up in prison over this, and they made a documentary about me, it would be kind of funny. Otherwise, it was just sad.

Though I couldn't say why, I thought about Nick. I kept thinking about him—down in that pit. Still alive and begging for help.

I crept up from behind, slow on the carpet. I never thought high school wrestling would matter much, but knowing how to do a proper sleeper hold was coming in handy lately.

And that was what I did. I shoved the gun in the band of my pants and wrapped my arm around Brent's thick neck. The poor bastard never saw it coming.

He bucked and tried to throw me, but he was a short guy and mushy around the middle. He weighed more than me, but sheer weight was all he had, and that wasn't worth much against my muscles. Besides, he was so surprised. Drunk and lost in his fantasy world of faraway murder, he never knew what hit him.

The TV droned in the background, a detective giving his two cents. *"We were dealing with a cunning predator who was able to elude capture for years. The killer was targeting isolated young women, making the case even more challenging."*

Brent gasped once more and passed out, and I dropped him back into his seat on the couch.

I cracked my neck and caught my breath. Then I took a minute to position Brent on the couch so he looked comfortable, natural.

I was ready for round two. I snatched up the remote in my gloved hand and turned the volume all the way up.

Taking out the gun, I sat down on the couch next to the unconscious man and pressed the weapon into his hand, careful to wrap his finger over the trigger. I lifted both of our arms and aimed the weapon at the hallway. And then, I waited.

"Brent?" Lily called, her voice cracking from sleep. I hadn't actually seen her in years, but I knew she'd recognize me.

She'd never liked me, never thought I was worthy of her time. I couldn't wait to see the look on her face when she walked in and saw me with her husband like this. My skin prickled with anticipation.

Footsteps padded down the hall from the bedroom, and she called for her husband again. "Brent! Turn it down!"

The TV was so loud, beating against my brain.

"In most cases, when I murdered these women, I did not know their names."

"What is going...?" As she stepped into the room, Lily cut herself off and froze in her tracks. As she took in the scene, her gaze locked on me, and her eyes widened.

She knew me.

"What the hell are you doing here?"

"I think you know." I steadied the gun and the weight of

Brent's limp arm with both of my hands, aimed, and fired a shot right between her wide eyes. Her body did a half twist from the impact before she fell silent and lifeless to the ground. I was really impressed with my shot, considering this was my first time firing this gun. Then again, I'd always been a pretty good shot. Guns just made sense to me.

The loud smack of the bullet through the suppressor shook Brent from his unconscious state, and he began to twitch and moan. I got off the couch, knelt in front of him, pressed the gun to his temple, and spattered his brains all over the Van Gogh sunflowers framed on the wall.

Immediately after squeezing the trigger, I let go so that his body would slump with the natural angel of the blast. He fell back, and the gun slipped from his right hand onto the carpet.

I left the gun right where it had landed. The boss had instructed me to do it just like that.

I was about to grab the remote to flick off the TV when I noticed dots of blood on it. I'd watched enough true crime myself to know I'd be in deep trouble if I smeared that blood, so I decided to just leave the TV on. Then I left the way I came, locking the door and the dead bolt behind me. That night, when I got home, I would file the key down, rendering it unidentifiable, before tossing it in the trash.

Just like the boss said. And I was nothing if not a model employee.

6

Winter yawned and poured herself another cup of coffee. She hadn't slept well the night before. The same dream haunted her, except this time, she was running along the black road searching for Tim, for the place where he was being sucked down into hell. But she couldn't find him. The road went on and on, and she woke up with a deep ache in her bones like she'd just run a marathon.

In that state, Noah's news that he'd be out of town for a few days did not hit her well. Of course she would miss him. She always missed him when he was away. But there was more to it than that. Winter would never say it out loud, but she didn't want to sleep alone.

"It's fine." She settled down into the breakfast nook across from Noah, first arranging her robe and then crossing her legs. "You don't need to apologize."

"I just told you I was going to be home from now on, and here I am going out of town. I feel like a liar."

"You'll make it up to me." She booped the tip of his nose playfully, hoping that would be the end of the conversation. She didn't want to talk about it anymore. If they did, she might accidentally admit her feelings, and then he might not go, and then she'd feel guilty.

Honestly, she was as deeply involved in the Grace Schumaker case as he was, albeit from a very different angle. She wanted that ring shut down as much as anyone. Noah was a wild racehorse, constantly jumping the gate. She'd never try to corral him and didn't envy his boss the job, but if she had to trust someone to do something and do it right, it was Noah.

Her husband got up from his seat, pausing to kiss her hair before ambling toward the bathroom.

Taking out her phone, Winter opened the app for her local newspaper. She wasn't a big fan of politics or world news or any of that other stuff all over the web that she could do absolutely nothing about, but keeping up with local goings-on was an important part of her job, which simultaneously fulfilled any civic responsibility she might feel.

Winter often thought that if people paid more attention to what was happening locally and less to what was happening everywhere else, the world would be a better place. It was far too easy to get scatterbrained and distracted in a global society. Austin was quite big enough for her tastes.

And she still read her favorite local rag from Richmond from time to time. Old habits.

She took a moment to digest an article about some construction plans for downtown—two blocks away from her office. In a couple of months, she was going to have a work zone to contend with on her morning commute.

Next, Winter checked the crime report—a separate section of the news site that was devoted to police calls, arrests, inmates, and details not included on TV broadcasts or the regular daily news. She read it nearly every day, especially when she was between cases.

Right at the top was a story about a husband and wife in their mid-thirties found dead in their home. The victim was local celebrity Brent Ballstow of Ball's Appliances, best known for starring in his own corny commercials.

A light bulb burst in Winter's head, and she slapped the table. "That's where I knew him from. He was the Ball Man!"

Granted, she hadn't been in Austin that long, but she had seen his goofy commercials on YouTube ever since her IP address moved into the Austin area. She could see his orange suit and hear his loud pitch in her head.

"I'm Brent Ballstow, owner of Ball's Appliances, and I am going Ball-istic cutting prices all over the store!"

"Holy shit." Once her brain managed to get over that hurdle, Winter zoomed in on the article. Brent and his wife of fifteen years, Lily Ballstow, had been found dead from an apparent murder-suicide. Brent had pulled the trigger.

"You doing okay in here?" Noah stepped back into the kitchen, pausing to give her a quirked eyebrow before padding over to the fridge in his bare feet.

"He was the Ball Man."

"So you said. I have no idea what that means."

"Brent Ballstow. I served him a summons Friday morning. He got really mad. Called me a fucking scumbag."

"What's that?" The vein in Noah's neck bulged and twitched. He closed the fridge and stepped toward her. "What happened? Why didn't you tell me about this?"

Winter dismissed him with a wave of her hand. "Nothing. I served him papers. Like a lot of people getting served, he wasn't happy. He even tried to grab me."

Noah's face went full-on gargoyle. "Did you break his teeth?"

Winter gave a little roll of her eyes, her lips pressed together. "I put him in his place. He was all bark, really."

"You've gone soft in your old age." He slipped onto the bench beside her and put his hand on her knee. Less than the feeling of an intimate touch, it was almost like he was trying to suit her up in armor.

"The report says he shot his wife and then shot himself. They're both dead."

"Oh, man. I'm sorry. That's messed up. I guess whatever you served him sent him over the edge."

Winter paled at the thought. Had she inadvertently killed two people by taking on some routine summons job?

Noah read her mind. "He was gonna get served those papers either way. Whether it was you or anyone else is immaterial."

She nodded along, knowing he was right. Still, something about it just wasn't sitting with her. "He mentioned someone called Nick to his wife, and she mentioned something about getting him in court. I don't know. I didn't hang around to chat."

Winter looked Brent Ballstow up on her phone and rooted around until she found one of his commercials to show Noah. As she watched it, she cut herself some slack for not recognizing him the other day. He was smiling like a cartoon in all his commercials—over-the-top and strangely charming, like only local business owners could be. His face had been like a stranger's yesterday. So much worry. And then the anger.

But also, she'd seen some tender love between him and his wife. There were many sides to the man. That was all she could really say with confidence.

"Huh." Noah sniffed when the video ended. "Umm. Did you get any vibes from him Friday?"

"I got plenty of vibes, but murder-suicide vibes? No. Not at all."

"Other than each other, you might've been one of the last people to see them alive."

Winter shuddered. That didn't sit well with her either. She read the original article through to the end, but there weren't many details. A neighbor had gone by the house to ask them to turn down their TV, which apparently had been thumping like EDM all night long. She'd knocked on the door, but no one answered. Eventually, she called the police, and that was when they found the bodies.

The police estimated Lily and Brent had died sometime around midnight. No witnesses in the neighborhood had yet been able to confirm when the shots were fired.

Noah made a little grunt to let her know he'd finished reading the article over her shoulder. "You'll have to go down to the station and give a statement."

Winter moaned as if in pain. "But Davenport is at the station."

Though they'd started on good footing, Winter's relationship with her self-elected police liaison, Detective Darnell Davenport, had been rapidly deteriorating. At first, he'd been impressed by her FBI credentials and seemed excited to work with her. But the more she was around, the more trouble she inadvertently caused him.

Noah sighed knowingly. "Between you and me, I think we've got every LEO in Austin mad at us. At this rate, we're gonna have to start wearing masks to fight crime."

Winter laughed, knowing he was talking about his SSA. "You said Falkner was being nice to you."

"It's a trap. I'm sure of it. He's trying to get me fired."

She wrinkled her nose. "Are you being serious right now?"

"I don't think so…"

Winter sighed and bumped her shoulder against his. "I guess we all have to face up sooner or later."

"Ain't that the truth, darlin'." He threw his arm around her. "I think you and me need a vacation. Maybe head off to the Bahamas or something. I'd love to see you in a bikini, playing on the beach."

"With whose money?" Winter snorted. "Tell you what. If you're a good boy, I'll take you to Applebee's."

Noah laughed deep in his gut and kissed her cheek. "I love you."

7

In a small conference room at the police station, Winter sat across from Detective Darnell Davenport, who sipped from a shiny black coffee cup. His extra-long limbs and neck made him seem taller than his six feet. The way he sprawled across his chair, legs akimbo, only accentuated the effect.

Since Winter had last seen Darnell, his face was hairier. Either he'd forgotten to shave for the past week, or he was in the process of growing a black goatee to match his tapered buzz cut. One index finger was pressed firmly into his temple, his dark eyes intensely focused as he listened to Winter give her statement.

She'd seen him smile before, ages ago. He had straight, brilliantly white teeth and dimples on both cheeks. A face naturally designed to smile made his scowl all the more unpleasant.

"Do you have any idea what the summons was for?" Darnell tapped his pen against his knee.

"I didn't read it. When Lily was talking to him, he mentioned the name Nick...?"

He frowned and let a long moment of silence slip by

before taking the bait. "Nicolas 'Nick' Riley. Thirty-two years old. Former salesman for Ballstow Appliances. Single guy, no kids. Grew up locally. Riley alleged in his suit that Brent Ballstow engaged him in a physical altercation."

"Meaning?"

"Ballstow slapped him upside the head and called him a moron."

Winter considered this for a moment, memories of Ballstow's blustering anger flashing through her mind. "I can see that."

"When Riley punched back, Ballstow became even more violent. Riley was suing for emotional and physical damages."

"How much?"

"Enough to ruin Ballstow and his business."

"Over one slap?"

"It wasn't just one slap. He broke Riley's wrist."

Winter fiddled with the plastic lid on her coffee cup before taking a slow sip. She could see that too. Brent Ballstow was a violent man with a bad temper. Still, he struck her as more of a Hank Hill type. Basically harmless, but occasionally threatening to kick people's asses and making good on it.

"A broken wrist? Ballstow would have to pay out for that even if he wasn't the Ballistic Ball Man."

Darnell nodded in agreement. "Makes sense he'd be in despair, especially after the news he got yesterday in those papers you gave him."

"What do you mean?"

"Riley somehow managed to get Wyatt Jones to represent him." He studied her, waiting for a reaction. She had none to give.

"Sounds like a…gunslinger?"

Darnell sneered at her sad attempt at a joke. "You're new around here, but Wyatt Jones is an institution. A bloodsucker with a capital B. With him on the case, Ballstow wouldn't stand a chance." Darnell twitched and sat forward. "How did he seem when you served him the summons?"

"Definitely despairing. And angry." Winter pushed out a heavy breath. "He demanded answers that I didn't have. Then, when I tried to leave, he grabbed my arm. I had to defend myself."

He dropped his hand so it landed with a dramatic thud against the side of his chair. "Don't tell me you got in a fight with him?"

"Not a fight. A minor incident. I put him in his place, and he stopped."

Darnell's scowl grew a new wrinkle. "Why is it I can't turn in any direction without running into you?"

Winter shrugged. Several facetious and ill-advised replies formed in her brain, but she managed to keep herself from saying any of them. "I'm just not sure this is as open-and-shut as you're making it out to be."

"Why? We got a local businessman on the verge of losing everything. About to be shamed and dragged through the mud in front of the whole community. Has a temper that even you just attested to. Remembers he has a gun in his safe and two bullets."

"It was his gun, then?"

"He's owned it for years."

"How were they found?"

"He was lying on the couch. It looked like he just called her into the room and, when she came…pow. Right between the eyes. She never saw it coming."

"While still sitting on the couch?" Winter raised an eyebrow. "That's one hell of a shot."

Darnell tapped his fingers on the table. "Granted, but the guy's owned guns for years and regularly went to practice at the range in his free time."

"Was he drunk?"

"We don't know yet, but there was a glass of whiskey found on the table next to the body."

Winter nodded, remembering. "He smelled like whiskey yesterday."

"There you go, then."

"If he was drunk and sitting down, that's an even more incredible shot."

"I can't say for certain the exact angle of the bullet just yet. He might've been standing right in front of her and then had a seat to finish himself off."

"Okay." What he said was logical, but Winter furrowed her brow, unconvinced. The whole thing was about as comfortable as a hangnail, rubbing her wrong from every direction. "And no forced entry?"

"All the doors were locked when we got there. We had to break in." Darnell stretched his arms out to the side with a muted groan, sighed, and folded them on his lap. "So Ballstow's life is falling apart. He's suffering from acute despair. Not thinking clearly. Very likely drinking. Substance abuse is a strong indicator in these kinds of cases."

Winter nodded again, but her face was pinched in thought. "And the TV was on with the volume turned all the way up."

"He was trying to cover the sound of the shots."

"That wouldn't really work."

"I know that, and you know that."

She set her coffee on the table, sighing in frustration. "If he was such a gun enthusiast, he'd know that too. I just don't think you should jump to conclusions."

"I never *jump* to conclusions," Darnell snapped, his pupils pinpricks. "I just explained, in far more detail than any civilian is entitled to, exactly why I'm considering this case the way I am. Why do you doubt my conclusion?"

It was a fair question. Winter wished she had a better answer than it just didn't sit right with her. Often when she had that feeling, it was simply a matter of her subconscious noticing things her conscious brain had bypassed. Figuring out why she felt the way she did was a matter of deciphering what she was actually thinking.

The PTSD brain was a curious thing.

Winter sat up straight. "But they were going away for the weekend."

Darnell opened his mouth and then closed it. "What?"

"They were packing up the RV to go away for the weekend. I saw the man loading groceries into it."

"So what?"

"So don't you think it's weird that a guy planning to kill himself and his family should bother going grocery shopping?"

"Maybe his wife did it. It was all her idea, so he just went along with it, knowing what he was planning on doing that night."

Winter's fingers curled into loose fists. "Okay, fine. Then why didn't they leave?"

"Getting it ready to head out in the morning."

"You wouldn't load up your perishables the night before. That's just illogical."

"We also noticed the RV had a flat tire. Two of them, I think."

"It did?" Pictures of the vehicle flashed through Winter's brain. It was one of those RVs that was sized and shaped like a city bus—bright white with a purple-and-teal swoosh on the side. Like those paper cups from the nineties. If the tires had been flat, she would've noticed. The whole thing would've been listing. "They weren't flat when I went by."

"What did you do, a safety inspection?"

"You think I wouldn't notice a flat tire?"

Darnell rolled his eyes. "Maybe Brent did it as an excuse not to go. He wanted to be at home when he died. Or maybe it was a spur-of-the-moment decision, made by a man who was unraveling."

Winter bit the inside of her cheek. Darnell was being deliberately obtuse now. Still, she felt compelled to plow ahead. "His wife is the other thing that gives me pause. I didn't get the impression she was at all frightened of her husband. Previous abuse is usually present in domestic murder-suicides."

He seemed like he was fighting very hard to not roll his eyes. "You never know what two people are like behind closed doors unless you're hiding in the closet."

"Granted, but when he yelled at me and grabbed me, she didn't seem scared. She didn't seem like a woman bracing for a fit of temper. In fact, she was all over him, in a sweet, almost motherly way. They were in their world, playing off each other like a couple in love." If Winter knew anything at all, it was how people who were truly in love reacted to one another.

"They'd been married for a while. Maybe she was used to it. Maybe she knew every trick to help her angry husband calm down. Or maybe she was just relieved to see it directed at someone else for a change."

"That's a lot of maybes."

"The guy has a track record for violence. He literally attacked you when you met him. It's not a stretch that he hit his wife." Darnell pointed his finger at her. "Besides, abuse isn't always present. Not physical anyway. Ballstow could've just killed her for the same reason he killed himself—to spare her the embarrassment of the inevitable fall from grace."

"Don't you think murder-suicide is a bit of an overreaction?"

"Yes. I always do."

Smart-ass.

Winter crossed her arms and looked away. "It just doesn't make sense to me."

Darnell stood and pushed his chair back in. "I appreciate you coming down here to give your statement, Winter. But unless there's something more concrete to add than your very insightful impressions, I'm afraid I have to get back to work."

Darnell, it doesn't have to be like this, she almost said out loud. A typical cop, he didn't give a crap about speculation, only evidence. She respected that point of view, but she'd seen the Ballstows. He hadn't killed his wife. "No. I don't have anything to add. Yet."

"Well, let me know when you do. Have a good rest of your day." He walked to the door, slipped through, and held it open. Winter snatched up her coffee and followed him.

The second she was through, he released the door and started off down the hall away from her. She almost called out to him but thought better of it. Every word out of her mouth seemed to irritate him. Besides, there was nothing she could say to change his mind about her or this case.

If she was going to convince Darnell to look into the Ballstow case more carefully, she would need something more substantial than uncomfortable feelings and a two-minute character analysis.

She needed proof.

8

That night, Winter couldn't sleep, so she got comfy on the couch with her laptop and emailed Ariel, giving her a barebones rundown of what had happened and tasking her with looking deeper into Brent and Lily Ballstow when she got into work in the morning. Then she started doing her own digging.

She told herself again and again that she was staying up late because of her niggling doubts about this case, not because she was scared of having another nightmare.

She almost believed it.

Luckily, there was a decent amount of press about the local businessperson. She rewatched all six of Ballstow's Ballistic ads, his over-the-top corniness hitting very differently than it had in the past. He was so smiley and loud—like the host of a kids' show or something.

When talking to Davenport earlier, she'd almost brought up the commercials as evidence that he couldn't possibly have committed these fatal crimes. But she'd thought better of it. He would've just given her another *you never can know* speech.

And he would've been right. In her line of work, she knew better than to judge a book by its cover…or a man based on his TV persona.

She found a few write-ups on him and his wife, Lily, in archives of the society pages from the local online newspaper. The most recent, from a little over a year ago, described Ballstow sponsoring a silent auction to rebuild a public swimming pool in his neighborhood.

Another article featured a picture of the couple—Brent in a black tux and Lily at his side in a flowing blue ball gown. Her black hair had been longer then, done up in twists and braids. And just like it had been two days ago when Winter met her at the house, Lily's makeup was thick, upstaging the rest of the photo. Her face was like a mask or a cartoon, especially with those fake eyelashes and thick liner.

In particular, the dark, heavy lipstick made her look a lot older than her age—only thirty at the time of her death.

The write-up itself didn't offer much new information. It mentioned that Ballstow had started the store on his own when he was only twenty-two years old. It also referred to Lily as a "JCH Bloom girl," though Winter had no idea what that meant.

She was about to search the term before she paused over another detail. The article described Ballstow as being "recovered from recent legal troubles." It was too old to have been talking about the case Nick Riley had brought, so that had to mean Ballstow had a different problem before.

Winter dug into the legal archives, searching for Ballstow under his personal name and his business name. It didn't take long before she found the case—Taylor Anderson versus Ball's Appliances.

Winter read the complaint. Like Riley, Anderson was another former employee. He'd worked in the back, doing repairs and operating the forklift. Last May, he had been badly injured when a refrigerator fell on him. His foot was broken, and he had to go to the emergency room and take six weeks off from work to heal. Ballstow was forced to pay out workers' comp.

The case alleged that when Anderson eventually did return to work, Ballstow claimed they'd had to downsize and that he and one other employee were being let go. Anderson claimed Ballstow had been looking for a reason to fire him before the accident and used the time off to replace him with a different hire.

The case of wrongful termination had been found for the plaintiff, and Ballstow was again forced to fork over a large settlement.

Thinking back to the *For Sale* sign in front of the Ballstows' picturesque home, Winter sent a second email to Ariel, this time asking her to dig deeper into their finances in particular.

Davenport had speculated that Nick Riley's case against the store could potentially ruin Ballstow—therefore giving him motive enough to put a bullet in his head. Now Winter wanted to put numbers behind the assumptions. How much had he lost on account of the Anderson case? Was he in debt, and if so, how deeply?

It seemed odd that a man who spent his life building up a business from nothing—and one who regularly gave back so much to his local community—would be willing to give up on everything over money, even a lot of money. From what she'd learned about him so far, Brent Ballstow seemed more the sort to pick himself up, dust himself off, and try again.

Or perhaps the money was not the source of his despair. Could it be the threat of public shame that moved him to act? When people found out he'd broken one of his employee's wrists, he was going to have to answer for that one way or another.

Winter closed her laptop and glanced out the front room window at the night sky. Though much of her view was obscured by streetlamps, looking out into the night cleared her mind and brought focus. Her next step would be to contact Nick Riley for his side of the story.

If she was going off the assumption that Brent Ballstow wasn't responsible for what happened, the next question was obvious. Who was? Who out there had a grudge against Brent and Lily Ballstow? What motivation did anybody have for wanting the two of them dead?

The one person she figured she could safely cross off the suspect list was Nick Riley. He had nothing to gain from Ballstow's death and a fair bit to lose. Then again, maybe he could still get his settlement from the store, even if the owner was deceased.

Would someone take over the store now to try to keep it open, or would Ball's Appliances be closing its doors permanently? It was a safe assumption that someone like Ballstow would have a will, probably simply leaving everything to his wife. But what would happen now that she was dead too?

Who stood to benefit from Brent and Lily Ballstow's deaths?

Tomorrow morning, she would head down to the appliance store and poke around for some answers.

It was past midnight now. Winter decided she needed to force herself to get some sleep. Or at least lie down next to Noah and close her eyes. Soon, he'd be off on his last mission before sabbatical, and without the security of having him in bed beside her, the prospect of sleep would become even more elusive.

9

Monday morning, Ball's Appliances was open for business. The assistant manager, a short, plump woman with exceptionally pale eyes, hair dyed Christmas green, and tulip-pink tips, was running around the store like a chicken with her head cut off. But when Winter introduced herself and explained why she was there, the woman took time to speak with her in the back office.

They stood beside a bank of used refrigerators in the process of being fixed up for sale, slick concrete underfoot.

"Can I get your name, please?" Winter asked, pen and notebook in hand.

"Cara Criver." She had a deep, nasally voice like something sticky was wedged in the back of her throat.

"I was so sorry to hear about your boss and his wife. I only met them once, but—"

"It don't make no sense." Cara punched one of the fridges lightly before turning to the side to rest her heavy shoulders against it. She was shaped vaguely like a chicken drumstick, heavy on top and thinning all the way down her legs to tiny, delicate ankles.

"What do you mean?"

"Brent would never. I just…" She swiped a tiny vape pen from her jeans pocket and took a drag, releasing strawberry-smelling vapor into the air. "I just can't believe it."

There was no way to tell if Cara's incredulity was justified, or if she was just in denial of the horror that had occurred so close to home.

"I understand he was having some legal troubles. Would you know anything about that?"

"You mean Nick?" She spat his name like a curse.

"Actually, I was more curious about Taylor Anderson. Were you working here when that whole thing happened?"

"Oh." She grunted. "I don't know. I don't want to speak ill of the dead or nothing."

"I understand. But anything you can tell me might help us understand exactly what happened to him and his wife."

"Poor Lily…" Cara shook her head at the ground. "She rubbed a lot of people the wrong way, but I really liked her."

Cara was clearly having a hard time focusing. Winter steered her back in the right direction. "Can you tell me a little bit about the trouble between Brent and Taylor?"

"I don't see how it matters now, but…Brent was a good man, and he was a good boss, but he was a bit of a cheapskate." Cara scuffed the floor with her shoe. "Taylor was kind of the unofficial backroom manager, and he was always hounding Brent about getting some more safety precautions in place. He especially wanted him to pay for steel-toed boots and back braces for all the guys. And new lifting straps, since the old ones were getting a bit frayed."

"How did Brent respond to Taylor's suggestions?"

Cara took another pull of her vape before turning it over in her hands, fiddling with the controls on the side. "Brent refused. It wasn't high on his list of priorities. So when

Taylor's strap broke and he hurt his toe, getting Brent to pay was kind of personal. You know what I mean?"

"Absolutely." Nodding, Winter took a step back to escape the sickly sweet smell of Cara's vape pen. But the appliances were packed so tightly, she couldn't go three inches before her ass ran into a chest freezer.

"And Brent knew that when Taylor came back, he was going to double down on everything he'd been nagging about ever since he started work. Brent didn't want to deal with it, so he canned him. That was a really bad idea, as it turned out."

"The report said another employee was let go at the same time?"

"Yeah. Fred, I think. Frank. One of those *fruh* names. He hadn't been working here long. I think he was about eighteen. We had him on register and working as a wipe."

Winter had no idea what a wipe was, but it didn't sound high profile. "Warehouse?"

"Cleaning the secondhand merch. I'm pretty sure he was stoned one hundred percent of the time he was working. Getting rid of him was a no-brainer."

"What happened to Taylor after he won the case?"

"He bought himself a house up in Michigan and retired."

Winter looked up from her notebook, eyebrow raised. "The settlement was that much?"

"Oh, yeah. Nearly put this place under. We're still barely getting by because of that."

Brent dug himself out of a deep hole once, Winter reasoned. Would he give up simply because it seemed to be happening again? "Do you know if Brent had hired a lawyer for the case against Nick Riley?"

"Yeah, he had a team. He said that last time he gave in too easy because he was scared of all the legal fees he'd end up with if he fought too hard. This time, he was going to spare no expense. He was determined Nick wouldn't see a penny."

Not the actions of a man in such a state of hopelessness he'd kill his wife and himself. More the actions of a man who had every intention of fighting this thing tooth and nail.

The avatar of Detective Davenport that lived in Winter's head vehemently disagreed. Maybe Brent Ballstow had started to fight, but when he learned about Nick Riley's fancy lawyer, he realized he could never win. And since he already knew just how dire the consequences of losing such a case could be, he decided to take himself out instead.

Winter turned her attention back to Cara Criver. "I was the one who served Brent the official papers regarding Nick's suit against him and the company. He was very upset."

"Wouldn't you be?" Cara scoffed. "Besides, Brent was already having a terrible day."

"How so?"

"He got real bad headaches sometimes. He had to go home early Friday 'cause he had a really nasty one coming on. Said he was just going to go lie down in the dark. I'm surprised he even got up to answer the door when you went over. He probably thought you were Lily."

Winter nodded right along just to help her keep talking, but then she wrinkled her nose in confusion. "Why would Lily be knocking on her own front door?"

"She lost her key a few days back. She came in here the other day and had to borrow Brent's to get into the house. They've been dealing with swapping the only key back and forth ever since."

"Too busy to get one made?"

Cara shrugged just as her phone buzzed in her pocket. When she pulled it out, she let out a heavy sigh. "I'm sorry. I gotta get back to work." She stepped through the door toward the showroom, leaving Winter to stew in Freon and other unpleasant smells.

10

Back at the office, Winter stabbed at her salad with far more aggression than the poor spring mix deserved. Her experience at Ball's Appliances had left her frustrated both with the case and with herself. She'd gotten Nick Riley's phone number from Cara Criver, but he hadn't answered, and his voicemail was full.

If she could just talk to Nick Riley, she felt like she'd have her answer as to whether this niggling doubt was worth pursuing. Brent Ballstow had broken his wrist, which made Riley a character witness like no other. If anybody could convince her Ballstow was capable of murder-suicide, it was that guy.

On the other hand, there was a large part of Winter— namely her bank account—nagging at the back of her brain to just drop the whole thing. When she'd returned to the office, Ariel had left a stack of briefs on her desk. Cases she'd picked out to pursue, just like Winter had asked her to. It was a stack of money, that was what it was. Easy money for the getting, if Winter could just focus on those, do the damn paperwork, and forget about Brent and Lily Ballstow.

She shoved a bite of lettuce and a cherry tomato in one cheek and chewed, picked up the top brief, and scanned it.

"Yada yada yada. Insurance fraud." Winter sighed and drummed her fingers on the desk. "Ariel?"

Her assistant was out front, tapping away at her computer. She glanced up, and hustled to Winter's office door. "What's up?"

"I was just wondering if you found out what a JCH Bloom girl is?"

"Yeah. One sec." She rushed back to her desk, snatched her tablet out of its holder, and hurried back in. Then she sat down in the brown leather chair across from Winter's desk. "JCH Bloom is a local cosmetics company, kind of like Avon and Mary Kay, sort of a *door to door saleslady* type of makeup line. Lily Ballstow was one of their top representatives."

"Mary Kay. Sure, they were an MLM. Still are, I think."

"Yes, and from what I can tell, so is JCH Bloom. Their offices are here in Austin, and they have one small store about ten blocks from here." Ariel scrolled down the page on her tablet. "But for the most part, their sales are done face-to-face. Each Bloom girl runs her own business and is responsible for hawking the products. They throw parties and do a lot of stuff on social media too. So yeah, its business paradigm is exactly multi-level marketing."

"Huh." Winter poked at her salad. "Did she make much money with it?"

"Like any MLM, if you're at the bottom, there's a good chance you're hemorrhaging money, but if you manage to get near the top, you're swimming in it. And Lily was actually the niece of the company's founder."

"And who would that be?"

Ariel flicked through her tablet for a moment. "The aunt's name is Jessica Huberth." She turned the tablet toward Winter, showing her a picture of Lily and another woman posing together at what looked like some kind of convention, lanyards with name tags hanging from both their necks.

Jessica looked to be in her forties, with a full face of expertly applied makeup and short, curly brown hair. She was uncommonly petite, her hourglass figure clad in a stylish-looking white pantsuit with strappy gold heels.

"Might be worth having a conversation with her. She must've known the Ballstows pretty well."

"You want me to get her number?"

Winter nodded and took another bite of her lunch. "But definitely keep digging into both Brent and Lily. And throw Jessica in there too."

"I take it you're not buying into the whole murder-suicide theory?"

"There's no logical reason why I shouldn't accept it. Other than those groceries." She groaned and let her chin fall against her palm. Darnell's theory that Lily had purchased them made perfect sense, unfortunately. "And a flat tire or two."

"Groceries? A flat tire?"

"Don't worry about it." Winter opened her laptop, pulled up the Tracers software, and typed in *Brent Ballstow* yet again. "Thanks for your help."

"No problem." Ariel turned and left.

It bothered Winter that the couple seemed to genuinely care about each other too. After Winter served Brent Ballstow with papers, Lily Ballstow had nothing but love in her eyes as she comforted her husband.

The results from the search engine populated. Winter was looking for any new updates on the case, but the second result in the list gave her so much more.

Nick Riley—ostensibly the reason Brent Ballstow had killed his wife and then himself—had been reported missing.

She clicked open the article. Apparently, the police had

found Nick's car parked on the highway shoulder, as if the car had fallen victim to engine trouble. The circumstances looked as if the driver would return any minute. There was old blood spatter on the seats and on the door. They were waiting for DNA verification. The police were not officially theorizing he was dead, but no one had seen him since last Wednesday evening, the day before locals said the car had appeared abandoned. There *was* speculation that Brent Ballstow was responsible for whatever had happened to him.

First, Ballstow assaulted Riley. Now it seemed he might have even killed him. The murder would've occurred before he took himself and his wife out, which happened late Friday night. The article hypothesized that Brent Ballstow might have been consumed by guilt and died by suicide over what he'd done or because he knew the police were going to catch him.

Winter sat back in her chair and tapped her fork against her knee in thought. It made absolutely no sense. Brent Ballstow was a fighter who had every intention of trying to beat this thing. Or at least, that was the impression she'd gotten from Cara Criver. He'd hired a team of lawyers, after all.

For the sake of argument, Winter imagined he did decide to kill Nick Riley. If so, it seemed far more likely he'd try to get away with it. He was a smart guy—a successful entrepreneur. Not your standard idiot murderer. He wouldn't have killed Riley in a fit of rage. He would've taken the time to plan the whole thing out. Hide the body, conceal the evidence.

If Riley disappeared, all Ballstow's problems would disappear with him. He seemed like the sort who would've at least tried to get away with the murder.

"Consumed by guilt..." Winter mumbled, reading over that section of speculative crime a second time.

So Brent Ballstow killed Nick Riley, thinking he'd try to get away with it. But his conscience couldn't take it. So to punish himself for the crime and to escape the pulsing of a tell-tale heart, he put a bullet in his own brain.

But if that was the case, why did he kill his wife?

"Because he doesn't want her to find out what he was like. He doesn't want to shame her. He doesn't want her to find out what kind of man he really was. He wants to spare her the pain of having to face all those pesky police interrogations. There are a lot of reasons…"

Winter poked her salad, thought about taking another bite, and set down her fork. She or any other investigator could stretch the facts to fit many theories, but that didn't make the facts of the case any less messy.

And it didn't change what she knew about Brent Ballstow as a person. Or Lily Ballstow, for that matter. They were fighters, go-getters. The kind of people who didn't feel compelled to give up so easily. It was no stretch to believe the man would kill Nick Riley. The stretch lay in thinking he wouldn't try to get away with it.

Moreover, she couldn't help but circle back to Lily soothing him in their driveway. They struck her as a happy couple—two people who faced the world side by side. People who shared love, commitment, even respect. The puzzle pieces didn't connect.

Winter glanced at the stack of briefs, knowing what she ought to spend the afternoon doing. Then she got back onto her computer and fell deeper down the Ballstow rabbit hole.

11

Winter sat at the kitchen table with her laptop open, but she wasn't really looking at the screen. Instead, her gaze was trained out the window, watching her husband. It was only March, and the chill had yet to leave the air, with intermittent rain sprinkling the city every day or so, but Noah had hauled out the grill to make Cajun honey-butter salmon and mixed veg.

Before going out, he'd thrown together a truly incredible chipotle guacamole, which Winter was munching like popcorn during a horror flick. By the time he got back inside, there might not be any left, not to mention, she wouldn't be hungry for the divine dinner he was creating.

She wasn't sure what kind of music he was listening to out there, but whatever it was, he sure was enjoying it. Noah sang under his breath and shook his booty as he basted the fish. It was definitely something nineties. Alternative rock and grunge were his jam if he wasn't listening to country. Maybe it was Soundgarden.

Smiling, Winter let her chin rest against her fist. Her

husband was six-four, built like a brick shithouse, and a certifiable deadly weapon. He was also cuter than a bug's ear.

When he walked around the side of the house to grab something for the barbecue, Winter sighed and turned back to her computer. She knew Noah would be going out of town tomorrow, and she really didn't want to think about that.

As she contemplated things she didn't want to think about, more and more came rushing in. She found herself typing the name *Opal Drewitt*.

She hadn't yet heard from Kline. In fact, since that first call from the police when she was informed her aunt was dead and her biological father was being held for questioning, she hadn't heard from anyone.

Winter's heart rate picked up as worries sprang forth.

When she'd spoken to the police, it hadn't seemed like Kline was in serious trouble. So long as he was innocent, and they hadn't found any further reason to hold him, he should've been out by now.

What if they'd found some reason to hold him? It did seem an odd coincidence that Opal died right after Kline went to visit her. What if he was involved somehow?

She pumped the brakes in her mind and did a hard one-eighty. She didn't want to think like that. But *Kline* wasn't even his real name. It was the name of a dead man.

But that was a hit and run accident. Yes, Kline had stolen the victim's identity and never reported the death to the authorities. He'd admitted as much. But what if he'd held something back?

"I hope you're hungry, darlin'," Noah boomed as he pushed open the screen into the kitchen, his hands full of trays piled with steaming barbecue.

Her stomach rumbled a response, despite all the guacamole in it.

Winter rose from her seat and cracked open a couple of beers as Noah dished out the food. As she sat down across from him, she inhaled the scent deeply. "This looks unbelievable."

Noah looked smug as he sat down. They dug in. The salmon was perfectly flakey, with a blackened char on the outside—spicy and sweet. Pure kitchen witchery. She plowed through half of the filet before she came up for air.

"Babe…" Winter glugged her beer. "Oh, my god."

He beamed with pride. "You ain't kiddin'."

"What the hell am I going to eat while you're gone?"

"You managed to feed yourself before we got hitched. How'd you do that?"

"I'd rather not think about it." She stabbed a tender round of zucchini on the end of her fork. "Micky Dee's, here I come."

He laughed. "Honestly, you gonna be all right here all on your own?"

"If anybody calls, I'll tell them you're in the shower."

His laughter faded. "I'm serious, Winter. With everything going on with Justin's fan club and with Kline and Opal…"

She took another drink to hide the tension in her face. "I'm a big girl."

"Have you heard from Kline yet?"

There he went, reading her mind again. Sometimes Winter wondered if, like her and her best friend, Autumn Trent, Noah might have a bit of sixth sense.

Or maybe he was just really good at his job.

Or maybe that was just what it was like to be in a healthy, supportive relationship.

Winter cleared her throat. "I've heard exactly nothing."

"And you haven't called to check?"

She bit the inside of her cheek and looked up at him from under her lashes. "Is that weird?"

"Is it weird for you not to get yourself personally involved in a case way outside your scope of influence? I don't know." He lifted his beer to his mouth. "Maybe we should ask Detective Davenport what he thinks."

"Smart-ass."

Noah smiled gently, the skin around his forest-green eyes wrinkling. "Speaking of Darnell, what did he have to say when you went in to give your report?"

"He seemed a bit exhausted just to be around me."

"You can hardly blame him."

"Excuse me?" She pressed her palm to her chest in exaggerated offense.

Noah held up his hands. "I know what it's like to have you constantly showing me up at work. Ain't fun."

She gave a long, slow, roll of her eyes. "Darnell thinks it was a murder-suicide. Open and shut."

"Clearly, you disagree." Noah washed down his food, set down his beer, and reached across the table for her hand. "Look, you told Davenport what you think, right?"

She narrowed her gaze at him and withdrew her hand. "Is that your bass-ackward way of telling me to back off?"

"Well, you don't have any skin in this game. You don't have a client. You're not being paid for it."

"Are you saying this because you're worried about money?"

He brushed off her question with an incredulous chuckle. "We got plenty of money to last the next little bit, and I have every intention of pulling some in even if I'm on sabbatical."

"Really? How do you plan to do that?"

"Don't change the subject." He squished his eyes shut, as if that would help him dodge her tangent. "We got enough in savings to pay the mortgage, rent on your office, and feed ourselves, but if Black Investigations isn't bringing any income, you won't able to keep Ariel on more than a couple of months."

Winter forced her jaw loose with a laugh. "You've got nothing to worry about. I've got a stack of paying cases lined up. It's not like I'm spending all my time thinking about the Ballstows."

That tasted bitter. Because it was a lie. She glanced at Noah—at his gentle, loving face—knowing he wanted nothing but the best for her. She couldn't lie to him.

"I'm sorry." Winter's tense shoulders deflated. "I don't know why I can't let it go."

"You have a bad feeling. I get it."

"I feel like that guy in that movie with the broken legs."

Noah scrunched up his nose. "What?"

"That famous old actor. The movie where he breaks both his legs and ends up staring out of a window day after day. He gets obsessed because he thinks his neighbor killed his wife. You made me watch it."

"Jimmy Stewart. *Rear Window*. Hitchcock. Classic." Noah picked something between his teeth with his pinky nail. "Why do you feel like Jimmy Stewart?"

Winter paused before answering. "I guess I'm just looking for something outside of myself to focus on. Something I can actually do something about."

12

Winter sat up with a painful gasp, clutching her chest. Her heart was beating so hard, her ribs vibrated like a xylophone struck by a hammer. Blistering tears pricked her eyes, and when she blinked, they rushed down her cheeks.

At her side, Noah mumbled in his sleep and turned over.

Winter got out of bed and rushed into the bathroom. She turned on the shower, stripped off her nightclothes, and climbed inside, where she crouched at the bottom of the porcelain tub. She wrapped her arms around herself and gently rocked back and forth, back and forth, the warm water drenching her like purifying rain.

She couldn't say how long she stayed like that. Long enough for her heart rate to slow down and for feeling to return to her numb fingers.

Tim's screams echoed in her ears as a creature—a homunculus wrapped in oily black clothes—drank the boy's blood from a golden cup. The horrifying image was burned into the backs of her eyelids. But, like an old photograph left in the sun, its face was a blur.

After seeing Noah off, Winter got in her Honda and drove toward her office. She didn't mention anything to him about her dream. If he knew just how bad her nightmares were, he might decide he was too needed at home to go off on his final farewell mission. It was as important to her as it was to him that he be there when they finished bringing down the trafficking ring. Besides, she was a big girl.

Speaking of traffic, Winter found herself stuck in it like she did most mornings. Austin was a great city in so many ways with its friendly locals, warm weather, thriving cultural scene, and world-class barbecue. But it did have a downside —bad traffic.

The day stretched before her, but her brain was still stewing over her nightmares. To try to pull herself away from them, Winter started making a mental list of what she intended to accomplish. With the weather so nice, she wanted to get out into nature. Maybe head over to El Barranco State Park and get on the rocks.

Of course, her equipment hadn't arrived yet. So that was out.

What she should've been doing was tackling that big pile of paying cases Ariel had lined up. Pay the bills, pay Ariel's wages, be a responsible business owner. All that jazz.

In the distance, she could just make out the familiar blue-and-red lights of a police cruiser. There was likely an accident up ahead, turning the highway into a parking lot.

Winter bit her lip and glanced at her phone, which was face down on the passenger seat. She wanted to call Davenport and ask him about the Nick Riley missing persons case. She had a strong feeling that when they got to the bottom of what happened to Brent and Lily Ballstow, they were going to find Riley.

Was it possible the disgruntled employee was angrier and far more dangerous than anybody had guessed? Maybe he got impatient with the legal system. Maybe his lawyer had given him some bad news. Either way, it was possible Riley decided the Ballistic Ball Man deserved worse than simply losing everything he'd worked his life to build. He deserved to die.

"No harm in just checking the news real quick." Parked behind a stream of cars, Winter picked up her phone, using facial recognition to unlock it. "I'm not wasting time. I ain't got nothing else to do right now."

She opened her browser and typed in *Brent and Lily Ballstow*, curious if there'd been any new updates since the last time she checked.

Nothing. Same old articles, the writers of which had so much confidence in the murder-suicide theory, they didn't even bother to toss in that all-too-important word *allegedly*.

Winter sighed, but her knee was shaking. She was so far out of the loop, she couldn't even guess at what the police were missing. Noah was right, though. Darnell was a good investigator. If there was something more, he'd get to the bottom of it.

Probably.

Eventually.

Though he'd get to it faster if she were helping him.

"You're being ridiculous," Winter admonished herself. "Let. It. Go."

Traffic began to crawl forward. She set her phone face down on the passenger seat. When a big semi merged out of the way, Winter caught a glimpse of the upcoming exit sign. The very exit she would take if she were going to the Ballstows' house.

She looked at the sign, at the car ahead of her, at her phone, back at the sign.

"Screw it."

Winter flicked on her signal, eased into a little opening, and took the exit off the freeway. She opened the map app on her phone and punched in the Ballstow's address to help her navigate through the tortuous residential area.

"Just a quick once-over. That's all. Then I'll go to work and spend the rest of the day doing boring stuff to make money. Scout's honor."

Convinced by her own banter, Winter let go of her guilt over the matter and refocused on the task at hand.

When she pulled up to the curb in front of the Ballstows' house, it looked different, even though not much had changed. The RV was still parked in the drive, but she could clearly see it leaning toward one corner. A vehicle she had never seen before was parked beside it—a nondescript beige sedan. A bumper sticker on the back proudly proclaimed, *Love Is My Religion*.

Winter got out of her Pilot and made her way toward the RV. She tried the door, which was locked, before stooping down by the flat tire.

Tires, plural. Two of them right next to each other, like on a long-haul truck. And both of them so flat that all the weight rested on the metal rims. Maybe Brent Ballstow had hit something big and popped them.

Or maybe somebody hadn't wanted them to leave.

Winter got down, setting her butt on the concrete, and scooched under the RV to check the surface of the deflated tires. She ran her fingers over the rubber on the first one, looking for a hole.

"Can I help you?"

Winter startled at the woman's voice and bonked her head on the under carriage. "Son of a…"

She pulled herself out from under the vehicle and rose to a stand.

The woman before her had a sculpted haircut—black, extremely short, and gelled in place. She was pushing six feet and was rounded like a top-heavy snowman. Her eyes were bloodshot, no makeup on her puffy face.

The woman held a thirteen-gallon black trash can with a very faint red glow emanating out. Winter's gift was calling out to her, telling to reach inside.

Her fingers twitched. She clenched them into a fist and forced herself to focus on the woman's face.

"Lily was a friend of mine." Winter kept her voice quiet, even adding the faintest tremble for authenticity. "I was just coming by to…actually, I'm not completely sure why I'm here. But then I saw the RV tilted like this and, next thing I knew, I was under it."

The woman's features softened. She set the can down on the driveway and offered her hand. "My name's Holly. Lily was my sister."

"Winter." She shook the outstretched hand, forcing herself not to stare at the garbage can. In her periphery, she saw it seemed to be full of recyclables—paper, cardboard, and tin cans. "I'm so sorry for your loss."

Holly nodded, silently accepting the condolences. "They finished cleaning up the scene yesterday." She sniffled, clearly holding back tears. She looked like she'd been crying for days on end. "I was going through Lily's things."

"Do you need any help?"

"Thanks, but I'm okay. They're dropping off one of those storage pods later today. My husband and his brother will be swinging by to move stuff."

Winter nodded. "I haven't heard much more about the case. Have the police figured out what happened?"

Holly wiped her eyes. "Everyone's convinced Brent did it. They won't listen to me."

Winter's ears pricked up at the anger in her voice. "You don't agree with them?"

"I don't know." She sighed so hard, it sounded painful. "I've known Brent for over a decade. He was a pain in the neck, but I just can't imagine him doing such a thing. He loved Lily so much. It was his main redeeming quality." Holly patted down her pockets—probably looking for a tissue to wipe her leaky nose—before turning back to the house. "I'll be right back."

"You want me to dump this for you?" Winter gestured to the can with the tip of her foot.

"Thanks." Holly offered a weak smile. "The blue dumpster alongside the garage."

Winter picked up the recyclables and headed down the lavender-lined driveway as Holly made her way back toward the porch. The second she heard the smack of the screen door closing, Winter set down the can and dug inside. Something wet got on her wrist, but she didn't stop until she clasped a paper outlined with the red glow.

It was a catalog of makeup, haircare, and skin products. Written across the top in curlicued lettering was *JCH Bloom*—all of it bathed in that red glow that only she could see, a beacon that told her this was important. This would lead her to the truth.

So much for intake paperwork. Winter shoved the catalog into her back pocket, hoisted the can back up, and dumped it.

13

I pulled up to the house just as some woman with long black hair was leaving. I didn't know who she was, and I didn't really give a damn. The boss mentioned that other Bloom girls might be swinging by, trying to move in on Lily's territory and snatch up her clients now that she was out of the picture.

And that woman definitely looked like someone who'd be pushing makeup. She said the company liked to cultivate that kind of dog-eat-dog competition among bottom-tier sales associates. The boss said not to worry.

But I *was* worried.

Worried about the scene I'd left behind, worried if I'd done everything right. Worried that Lily—or even Brent— had somehow suspected what was going to happen to them and left a trail of clues to lead the cops right to me.

I'd followed the boss's instructions to the letter. She always said that was the best thing about me. I was a good listener, and I knew how to do what I was told. Like a dog, she said. But she always said how much she liked dogs.

The boss had told me to leave the gun in Brent's hand or

let it fall out naturally, to not clean up at all, and to lock the door behind me when I left.

I'd worn gloves and kept my hair hidden under a bandanna so I wouldn't leave any trace. Nobody had to tell me to do that. Not unlike Brent Ballstow, I'd seen my fair share of *Forensic Files*. I knew all about leaving pieces of yourself behind and taking pieces of the scene with you. All about patterns in blood and hair follicle analysis. I also knew some of the subtler rules about how to get away with murder.

Rule number one—don't kill anybody you know personally. And if you did know them personally, make sure there was no obvious motive why you'd want them dead.

Motive is king when it comes to murder.

I mean, technically, Lily and I knew each other. But that was a different time and in very different circumstances. The last time I saw her was at a family reunion five years ago, and we hadn't even spoken then. Our eyes met once over the potato salad, and we mutually decided we had nothing to say.

If Lily or Brent ever did think about me, it was probably just to thank their stars they never had to see me again. I gave Lily the creeps, apparently. The boss told me that once.

The investigators all seemed convinced Brent had done the deed, which had been the point, of course. It was just good luck he had a reputation for being violent and a little off his rocker.

I guessed it made sense I'd be worried, though. This was my first time killing somebody on purpose. I didn't count Nick, since I hadn't planned on killing him. It wasn't my fault he hadn't seen that well...as *well* as he should have. Stupid bastard had to go get himself killed.

At least, I thought he'd be dead by now.

It'd been a week, and I was pretty sure he'd hurt his leg

bad in the process. There was some water down there, I guessed, but drinking it only would've made him sicker.

Nonetheless, I knew he was still alive down there. Every night, I heard him screaming and scratching at the walls. Even with my swamp cooler and my generator running twenty-four seven, I heard him. I didn't understand how he could be so loud. His voice was like an ice pick driving into my ear and through my brain.

I wished he'd just hurry up and die already. With the way he kept hollering and begging, I'd have sworn I hadn't gotten more than two winks since he fell down there.

Night after night, I imagined going out there, throwing open the lid, and emptying a couple of shotgun shells into the well. And night after night, I simply couldn't bring myself to do it. I didn't want to see him down there, covered in that filth, rotting away. And I sure didn't want to smell him.

A shiver ran over my shoulders. I flicked on the heat in my truck to chase it away and turned my attention back to the Ballstows. The yellow crime scene tape was gone. That was a good sign. It meant the cops were all done going through the scene and everything was now being cleaned up. Another woman was still there, moving things around inside. It took me a while to realize who she was. She'd put on a fair amount of weight since I'd seen her last.

Holly, Lily's older sister. She was taller and wider than Lily, but there was no mistaking the family resemblance. She was also a busybody of epic proportions. Back when I'd known her and her sister, she was always the one sticking her nose in my business and making judgments about every little thing I said and did.

Now that I was looking at her, I wished Holly had been the one killed instead of Lily. Then again, Holly never would've let herself get involved in such nasty business. She was smarter than Lily. Knew when to stop, and she wasn't greedy.

She always was the smart one.

I wondered if she bought the story I'd set up at the crime scene. If someone who knew Brent well was convinced he did it, then I had nothing to worry about.

Still, there was something about this whole scene that didn't sit quite right. For starters, I didn't understand why the boss had told me to kill them in the first place. Once Nick was out of the picture, what difference did Lily and Brent really make? They could've been easily silenced with a payout.

Both of them were greedier than squirrels in October, though. That was what the boss said. And that we'd be living with targets on our backs. Sleeping with one eye open. Waiting for the other ball to drop. Or was it a hat that dropped? I couldn't remember all the catchy phrases she used to justify killing them.

I had noticed the boss was getting greedier too. Taking more risks, cutting more corners, getting stingier. Had I killed two people just 'cause she didn't want to part with any cash?

Best not to worry about it too much. In the end, it'd all be worth it. As soon as we cleaned up this situation, she promised we could close up shop and retire somewhere overseas—somewhere sunny and warm. White, sandy beaches and crystal-blue waters. A hammock for two strung between two palm trees. It wouldn't be strictly business. We'd finally be free to just be together.

My lonely heart grew two sizes, just dreaming about being with her all the time. But still, it ached knowing there was more work to do. The boss had called this morning and told me the next step. More business, more ugliness. More of the grisly work that would finally buy us our freedom.

I sat in silence as the sister picked up a cardboard box full of trinkets and loaded it into her trunk. Then she got into the driver's seat, pulled out, and sped away. I had nothing to fear. If anything, I was creating trouble by stewing on all this, thinking about entering the premises.

The boss would be pissed if she knew I'd even considered it.

Days had passed. The cops had finished with the crime scene. I needed to focus on the road ahead and move on.

But I was so tired. My brain was getting foggy. And back at home, all I had to look forward to was more screaming. It made that shotgun idea of mine sound better and better.

Nick had to be dead by now. He just had to be.

14

By three o'clock, Winter had closed two paying cases, making her feel less like an obsessive amateur sleuth and more like the licensed business owner she'd set herself up to be.

Seated at her desk with her third cup of coffee, she cracked her knuckles and began hunting through the briefs for another easy case.

Ariel tapped on the open door and stepped into her office. "There's a woman on the phone who's very insistent about speaking to you."

"Who is it?" Winter asked without looking up.

"She says her name is Suzannah. She wants to talk to you about custody of her nephew, Tim."

Winter's heart skipped a beat, stumbling over the rhythm. She grew lightheaded as the blood drained from her face.

"Are you okay?"

When Winter tried to answer, her voice cracked. She cleared her throat. "I'll take the call."

"Line two." Ariel stared for another moment, looking very

concerned. Then she turned on her heel and headed toward her desk.

Sitting back in her seat, Winter stared at her big, clunky office phone. The little green light on line two blinked. She took a deep breath and picked it up. "Winter Black speaking."

"Hello, Mrs. Black. My name is Suzannah Hall-Tolle. Thank you very much for accepting my call." The voice was deep and earthy, an upper-class Southern accent. Winter immediately pictured her sitting on a verandah, drinking sweet tea.

"Of course. What can I do for you?"

"I hope I'm not interrupting anything. I would very much like to speak with you about some concerns I'm having regarding my nephew's custody. Timothy Stewart. I understand you were intimately involved with the circumstances that left him an orphan." She gave the tiniest cough, as if there was too much lemon in that tea. "I thought you might be uniquely qualified to help me."

"I would do anything to help Tim." The words came out before Winter really had time to consider them, but they rang true as gospel. "Is everything okay?"

"Frankly, no, Miss Black."

"Mrs. Black-Dalton."

The older woman clicked her tongue and hummed as if she'd just heard bad news about the weather. But she proceeded more respectfully. "Everything is not okay. In fact, nothing is remotely okay. I'm incredibly distraught over my nephew's well-being."

So am I.

"Why is that?"

"Timothy's mother, Andrea, was my baby sister. We were never exceptionally close, and before her death, we hadn't spoken for years. I was not informed of what had happened to my sister and her family until after Timothy had already been liberated from the clutches of that godless monster and been delivered into the hands of his uncle, Guy Hall."

"I'm sorry for your loss."

"The Lord works in very mysterious ways." Suzannah sniffled. "Ours is not to try to understand, but to accept with grace and always strive to do his work."

"Of course," Winter said politely, all the while thinking, *Whatever you say*.

"I'm calling you today because a savage miscarriage of justice has taken place."

Winter's eyes widened at the strong words. "What do you mean?"

"Guy Hall is unfit to be the boy's guardian. It is absurd that Timothy was placed with him in the first place, given his record. I blame myself for not keeping contact with my family, but that does not mean I'm going to allow this to stand."

Winter straightened in her chair. "Why do you think Guy's unfit?"

"I'm not one to speak ill of my own brother. Gossip is the product of depraved minds. But on this matter, I cannot keep my silence." Suzannah's tone grew strident. "Guy is a man with many demons, one of which is alcohol. He's been arrested on more than one occasion for driving while under the influence and for public exposure of himself while under the influence. And he's had altercations with police. Physical altercations."

"Really?"

Winter's nightmare bubbled back to the surface like butter spattering from a hot skillet. Could this be what her unconscious mind had been trying to tell her? Was Tim unsafe where he was right now? Was Uncle Guy the oily, black, blood-guzzling homunculus from her dream?

"Did Greg and Andrea give custody of Tim to Guy in their will?" she asked.

"I can't imagine Gregory doing anything with such forethought. I know now that the authorities made an effort to contact me at the time Timothy was in state custody, but they were unable to get through."

"And why is that?"

"I live mostly off the grid, you see. And I tend to go by my late husband's name, Tolle, not my maiden name, Hall." She sighed heavily. "I believe Timothy was placed with Guy simply because he was the only relative they were able to locate."

Icy pins spread through Winter's chest, her heart squeezing painfully. "Have you contacted Guy about this?"

Suzannah began to groan, then cleared her throat to stifle it. "I've made several attempts to appeal to my brother's reason, but he's been incredibly unresponsive. He's very self-centered and entirely godless. I fear he does not have a conscience to appeal to."

That was a rather harsh accusation, but Winter had no evidence to refute it. She had only met Guy Hall once, when Tim was first placed with him. He'd been curt and unfriendly, as aloof as he was tall. He had also seemed like a perfectly respectable and contributing member of society. Clean, well-dressed, intelligent.

Winter couldn't remember exactly what he did for a living—something with finance—but he was incredibly well-off and lived on the outskirts of San Antonio. She also knew he had no kids of his own and had never been married.

"What are you looking for from me exactly?"

"I want to hire you to help me find proof that Guy is an unfit guardian so I can gain custody of my nephew." A twinge of softness entered Suzannah's voice. "I was never able to have children of my own, you see, and I feel like I'm being called to bring this young man into my life. To take care of him and help him heal from all the misfortune he's endured."

Misfortune seemed an understatement, like calling the Atlantic Ocean a bit damp.

"I cannot stomach the thought of poor Timothy being in Guy's care. There's no doubt in my mind he's being neglected. And I can't imagine he's being given all the resources a boy like him needs to thrive. I need you to surveil Guy Hall, prove he's unfit, and help me gain custody of my nephew."

The idea of taking Suzannah Hall-Tolle on as a client made Winter uneasy. She didn't want to take any side in this other than Tim's—to help make sure he had the best care possible.

"I'm happy to help in any way I can, but the work I do is evidence-based. So I can't approach this investigation hoping to find proof that Guy's an unfit guardian. I wouldn't feel comfortable taking you on as a client if your goal is to find dirt on Guy Hall. I can, however, do my best to uncover the truth. I only want what's best for Tim."

"As do I." The emphasis Suzannah put on each word was like a drill in Winter's ear. "Does that mean you'll investigate Guy?"

"Yes, I will. For Tim's sake."

"I'm very relieved to hear you say that. But I warn you, Miss Black, you are not going to like what you find." Something about Suzannah's drawling voice made those words sound even more ominous. "I'll be waiting for your call."

15

Colleen Sturgis was waking up from her midday nap after coming down from her morning high. Blinking in the afternoon sun, she needed a few seconds to recollect where she was. Home, in her living room. Exactly where she was supposed to be.

Tremors danced over her skin, forcing her to sit up. She snatched up a fluffy white sheepskin draped over the back of the chaise lounge and threw it over her shoulders. A foul taste coated her mouth—bitter and acidic all at once.

Her beautiful six-bedroom home sparkled with her interior designer's impeccable taste. Overhead, a modern chandelier—comprising several dozen wrought iron triangles woven together into a huge ball—scattered warm light across the ceiling. For days now, she'd forgotten to switch it off.

Colleen slid a small, lacquered trunk on the glass coffee table toward herself and opened the lid. Inside were a few pre-rolled joints, a plastic bag of MDMA powder, pill bottles full of uppers, downers, painkillers, and muscle relaxants, a large balloon of heroin, her dwindling supply of crystal, and a tiny sheet covered with smiley face emojis—each one a dose of LSD.

It was time to refuel—Vyvanse to get her moving and progestin for her premenopausal hot flashes. Then she did a small bump of cocaine, lit a cigarette, and hobbled across her mahogany floors. Her pedicure winked in the sunlight as she made her way into the kitchen.

Her stomach felt like it was stuck to her backbone, the physical sensation of hunger so painful that her knees shook under her. How long had it been since she last ate?

Two or three days, maybe. Ever since she'd heard about what happened to Lily, Colleen had been keeping herself distracted. She hadn't wanted to think about the implications. She really hoped it had all gone down exactly like the police said—that Brent had just gone crazy and killed her and then himself. The other possibility was too terrible to think of.

"Loose lips sink ships." That was what her father used to say. Colleen was disgusted with herself for ever letting Lily cajole her into helping with her money-grubbing crusade. All out of a desire to keep her loose cannon of a husband out of the poorhouse.

The only way anybody would know about Colleen's part in Lily's blackmailing coup was if Lily herself had spilled the tea just before somebody—hopefully, Brent—put that bullet in her brain. Lily always had loose lips. Loose lips, loose tongue, and a runny brain convinced of its own invincibility, despite spending her whole life in the damn suburbs.

But Lily was also fun to be around. And she had a way of making a person feel like they mattered. Colleen hadn't had a real friend in years. Lily popping over to persuade her to give up information about the company was annoying. Yet it made Colleen feel needed, something she hadn't experienced in a long time.

All she'd done was give Lily an address, that was all. An address she might easily have found herself by hiring any two-bit P.I. What could be the harm in it?

Or at least, that had been Colleen's reasoning before Lily and her husband turned up dead.

For days now, Colleen had felt like somebody was watching her. There were eyes around every corner and in every patch of darkness. The question ran through her brain over and over on a loop. Had Lily waggled those loose lips of hers before she was silenced forever?

Hopefully, it was the cocktail of drugs in her system making her paranoid.

Colleen shoved a coffee pod into her coffee maker, pushed *Brew*, and staggered over to her fridge. She caught her reflection in the sheen of the glass cabinets. Her short white hair, which she usually kept styled in curls, was sticking up in every direction like Einstein. She could hardly believe the size of the bags under her eyes.

When she was in her early thirties—back when she was broke and sharing a rathole apartment with four other people—she used to wake up after a bender, see the faint hint of gray under her eyes, and cry that she was getting old. Then she would slather her face with a full trowel of makeup.

Now in her fifties, the puffy bags were bigger than her eyes. She had the money to pay for Botox, fillers, or plastic surgery—any of the ingenious methods humans used to try to stay young. But Colleen couldn't bring herself to give a shit, other than to sigh and turn away from her reflection.

She pulled some leftovers from the fridge to make a sandwich, cutting thin slices of the roast she'd made before she'd gotten the news about Lily.

A heavy thud outside made her jump. The knife slipped and sliced through the tip of one finger.

"Son of a…" Blood oozed from her skin, decorating her sandwich like a swirl of ketchup on top of the mayo. Colleen hurried to the sink and ran the wound under a cool tap before wrapping the finger with a wad of paper towels. Then she gazed, crestfallen, at her contaminated sandwich. She'd have to start all over again.

She realized she'd used up the last of the brioche and had to go into the pantry to fetch out more bread. All she had left was gluten-free, ancient-grain healthy crap with the texture of wet sand. It was like rubbing salt in the wound.

When she was sober, she had told her personal shopper to fill her cabinets with healthy food so that when she got high, she wouldn't be able to stuff her face with Twinkies and chips. Her swollen ass would thank her. But here and now, she cursed herself. She didn't want to eat any of that rabbit food.

She headed back to the kitchen, where she was startled by another thud. This time, it didn't sound like it was coming from outside. It was in her living room.

Her heart knocked out a timid beat, and she snatched up the slender, pointed French butcher knife. Though fear spread through her veins like pins and needles, she held her breath and listened intently. Knife poised, she tiptoed to the edge of the kitchen and peered into the room.

Her little lacquered medicine box sat open on the coffee table. Prisms hanging in the window scattered rainbows throughout the room. Everything was exactly as she'd left it.

Sighing in relief, Colleen lowered the knife. Her stomach grumbled, willing her back to the kitchen.

When she turned, a man stood right there, two feet in front of her, his six-foot frame silhouetted by the light. As Colleen screamed and raised the knife, she fixated on the faded red bandanna on his head, recognition dawning.

"Fobbie? What the hell? You scared me half to death."

He didn't respond to the nickname she'd given him back when they were kids. He had a look of terror in his eyes, and that was when Colleen knew. He was the one who killed Lily.

She raised the knife again to plunge it into his chest.

He caught her hand as the knife came down and twisted her wrist around. Her bones popped as the knife plunged right through her flesh.

Colleen screamed in pain as she stumbled back, the knife protruding from her stomach, her hand hanging awkwardly from a broken wrist.

She looked down at the knife, appraising the damage with curiosity before the pain from the stab wound smacked into her consciousness like a freight train. She turned to run but stumbled onto her hands and knees.

Fobbie snatched her by the hair, yanking her up. He ripped the knife out of her stomach and plunged the blade into more soft tissue at her side. Then he pulled it out and stabbed her higher—the tip sliding between two ribs. He let go of her hair after that, and she fell back down.

Colleen tried to scream, but her lungs heaved, filling with blood. Her clothes turned dark as her wounds spouted red, a puddle spreading from her body across the floor. The blood was hot on her skin, but her body trembled with cold. She reached for her attacker and clamped her fingers onto the cuffs of his jeans. He kicked her off and walked away.

The moment she'd heard Lily and Brent had died, Colleen should've known she was next. But she hadn't bothered to prepare herself. She'd gone into denial, pretending none of this was happening—that it could never happen to her.

And Fobbie was a scumbag, sure. A thief and a drug dealer, absolutely. But not a murderer. This wasn't him. No matter what she'd done.

Colleen spasmed, pain shaking into the farthest corners of her body.

She would've given him everything her dead husband had bequeathed her. Anything to save her own life. Her entire fortune, if that was what it came to. If only he'd given her the option.

Just as she was trying to remember where her phone was to call 911, he came back and just stared at her.

She was going to die if she didn't do something, but what? How could she call 911 with him there? But if she didn't, she'd bleed out. So much blood was already soaking into her pristine white rug. She pressed her hands into the floor, trying to force herself up. Blood spurted from the wound on the side of her chest, and she dropped.

Gurgled grunts and screaming sobs tore from her throat. She tried to speak, tried to beg Fobbie to help her.

Was he…crying? He tilted his head like a curious dog, tears littering his cheeks, as he watched her fumble and writhe.

Colleen attempted to scream, to ask him why he was doing this, but all that came out was bubbles of blood.

After an eternity, he stepped back.

Colleen collapsed on her other side and tried to curl into a ball. She was so cold. The pain was beginning to fade like the memory of a dream, leaving nothing behind but the bone-chilling ice. She needed a blanket and pillow, a chance to take a nap. She couldn't remember the last time she'd felt so tired. But her skin was starting to warm up. At least there was that.

Gently, Colleen let her head rest on the cool tile. All she needed was to close her eyes for a few minutes, and soon, she'd be right as rain.

Just a few minutes.

16

The boss told me I needed to *stage the scene* with drugs. But I knew that wouldn't be necessary. Colleen had more drugs sitting in her fancy little chest than I'd brought with me anyway. And I already knew—because me and her went way back—that she had more stashed in different little hiding places around the house.

I thought it was kind of weird the boss wanted me to leave a bunch of drugs all over the place. Usually, it was better to do the opposite, especially when breaking into a nice house like this.

If it were up to me, I'd have tried to make this look like a robbery gone wrong. I'd have gone through the house, taken all her jewelry and her silver. Tried to bust open that safe I knew she kept in her bedroom. Maybe unhook the various TVs she had all over and stack them by the front door.

But the boss knew best. I wasn't even smart enough to understand why we had to kill Colleen in the first place. Yes, I knew she told Lily about the company, but Colleen was never ever going to go to the cops about anything. And she sure as hell didn't need to blackmail us for money.

Lily had threatened to destroy everything. I knew her death was necessary to protect everything we'd worked for. And her husband had to die for the same reason—so he wouldn't dig too deep into his wife's death and expose everything.

And Nick? That plan went sideways…

Nick was still down in that well, still screaming. Still begging. It didn't make any sense. Nobody could survive that. Nobody.

I sure wish he'd just die already. If the boss finds out he's not dead, I'm going to be in a heap of trouble.

But why did I have to kill Colleen? Shit, I couldn't stop crying.

The company was launched thanks to her seed money, financed by Colleen's stash from her dead rich husband. That had to have meant something. But the boss said no, made it very clear that she didn't keep me around for my brains too. The woman didn't even trust me to tell a joke right.

Now that Colleen was gone—our "final loose string," as the boss called her—we could skip out of Texas entirely, never come back. She'd warned me that meant leaving my sons behind. I would miss them, but the sacrifice was necessary for me to be with the boss. I'd leave the house to Troy and Mike, along with a big chunk of my share of the money.

Knowing my boys, they'd probably blaze through it all in a week, but that wasn't the point. The point was I'd done my fatherly duty. Because once me and the boss jumped ship, I had no intention of ever looking back.

I'm really going to miss my boys when all this is over, though.

I had to sit down.

All this emotion running through me was exhausting. But I couldn't sit, so I paced around the kitchen, but my eyes just kept going back to her.

I walked over and crouched. "Hey, Colleen, I'm really sorry about your murder."

Blood pooled all around her, and the way her mouth was frozen—lips parted but with a little curve—made her look like she was grinning. *"I forgive you, Fobbie."* I could almost hear her saying it.

The more I studied her, the more I noticed how rough she looked, and not 'cause of me. She looked like an old cow skull stuck in the desert and then bleached white by the sun. Colleen had always loved laying out. That was why her skin had the texture of shoe leather.

I first started dealing drugs back in junior high when I realized just how much I could sneak from my mom's stash without her noticing. It was mostly weed and cocaine in those days. Once I started buying for myself, though, I'd get ahold of some PCP from time to time. That was Colleen's favorite.

"Do you remember that, Collie? How much you loved that shit? How you used to throw yourself at me, begging to fuck me in exchange for your next fix?" I shook my head at Colleen. "The good ole days."

The pool of blood was creeping out in all directions. It was still coming out of her. Fascinating. I got back up and stepped away. She'd taken a long time to finally die, even after she passed out. I'd considered stabbing her a fourth time, but instead, I just stood back and watched.

It was amazing just how resilient the human body was. Just like how everything you saw in Hollywood about suppressors was total bullshit, so was a bad guy biting the big one from a single smack across the head. I'd seen it firsthand with Colleen—just like I kept hearing it with Nick, night after night after night. The body fought to stay alive long after it should give up.

When she recognized me, maybe I should've given her a

chance to speak. I didn't want to hear what she had to say, though, didn't want to listen to her beg. Every time I closed my eyes and started to drift off to sleep—no matter where I was—I had to listen to that whiny, worthless guy beg for his life.

"Help me! Help me! Let me out!" The same thing every time. Night after night, moment on top of moment.

I couldn't bear to add Colleen's voice to the cacophony. Even if she was dead, and I could see that with my own eyes, I didn't want to have to listen to the echo of her pleading for her life.

"Fobbie, help me! Please!" Saying my name and reminding me that we'd been friends for decades.

When I looked at Colleen all dried up on the tile—old and rich and dead—I saw the fourteen-year-old girl with goth makeup all around her eyes. That girl was basically good, if a little traumatized from living with an unpredictable, schizophrenic mother who never should've had custody of her in the first place. I remembered how she used to cut herself. How she used to cry.

I also saw the pathetic drug addict Colleen became. I saw the stripper who took customers home at night if the price was right. The woman who had an affair with a married man thirty years her senior, then pretended to be pregnant so he'd divorce his wife and marry her.

The poor bastard died only a few years later. I sometimes wondered…

Colleen was a disgusting person, but she had also been my friend.

The boss had to believe I was loyal now. She had to know I'd do anything for the plan. I'd murdered my oldest friend, for whatever that was worth, and for no reason other than the boss wanted me to.

I looked around the kitchen. Colleen had been making

lunch when I arrived. She needed it, too, with how all the drugs she always put in her system made her so malnourished.

Smelled like she'd brewed some coffee too. The scent hovered over the stink of death, now that I was concentrating.

"What exactly were you making, Collie?"

I went over to study the sandwich. Roast beef and pickled onions. Nothing I ever would've made for myself, but I could tell she'd really been making it with care. Almost like she knew it was going to be her last meal.

That brioche bread was high end. And it was smothered in that froufrou pink mayo. Maybe it was sriracha. She'd really overdone it with that, though. "That's not good for your cholesterol, girl."

But last meals were about pleasure, not calorie counting. The least I could do was enjoy it for her.

I took a bite. The bread was fluffy and sweet. And that pink sauce had this nice kinda coppery tinge to it. Or maybe that was the roast beef. In any case...

"This is a fantastic last meal. You did good, Collie"

I finished the sandwich as an homage to my old friend, but my stomach hurt immediately afterward. Probably all that damn fancy mayonnaise. I wasn't used to sucking down so much fat so quickly. That coppery taste was coating my tongue now. I grabbed a coke from the fridge—still with my gloves on, of course—and tried to wash it down.

The taste wouldn't budge. I needed to brush my teeth.

Before I left, I crouched down beside Colleen, balancing on the balls of my feet.

"Goodbye, Collie. I've got my memories, but I don't know that anyone's really gonna miss you. You burned bridges with that daughter of yours so long ago..."

I thought about that little girl, how Colleen used to drag

her around with her as she looked for her next fix. I
wondered if I ought to try to find her and tell her about her
mom. I knew she'd disowned Colleen a long time ago. I
wasn't her only dealer, of course, and when Colleen used to
offer her daughter up in exchange for drugs, that was where I
drew the line, but I knew there were some guys who
accepted her child in trade.

"Maybe it's for the best you're dead. The world ain't
gonna miss you, Collie, just like it won't miss me in the end.
But unlike you, I actually have a chance to be happy. Can you
blame me for taking it? I know you'd have done the same,
given the choice. I just know you would have."

I brushed my fingers lightly over her eyelids to close
them. Then I pushed to my feet. All I had to do was keep
playing my part. The boss had a plan, and I knew that in the
end, it would all work out and everyone would win.

Except Colleen, of course. And Lily. And Brent. And that
Nick guy stuck down the well.

"You know this was nothing personal." I took another sip
of my coke and burped on the fizz. "Personally, I would
never kill anybody. I'm not a killer. You know that."

With a final glance at the pool of blood and my sad old
friend lying like an island at its center, I turned my back and
left the house through the back door, putting the key under
the mat where I'd found it. She probably had another key
hiding under the mat at the front door, too, and maybe one
on a chain around her neck. Poor dumb druggie.

I needed to call the boss and let her know the job was
done.

She was gonna be so happy.

17

Winter fried up the leftover vegetables from Noah's barbecue, poured them over a bowl of ramen with a boiled egg, and sat down at the table to eat. But staring at the empty spot where Noah was supposed to be just made her think about how she was going to be sleeping alone tonight. Instead, she got out a tray, set herself up in the living room in front of the TV, and put on an episode of her new favorite show, one of the latest *Star Trek* iterations.

Patrick Stewart was still sexy even at eighty. How was that even possible?

For the first ten minutes, her focus was on eating, but as the noodles filled the hole in her stomach, she found her attention wandering. She pulled out the catalog she'd taken from Lily's recycling bin—the one that had beckoned her with a red glow—and perused the offerings.

Every page was filled with colorful photos of beautiful women wearing all shades of lipsticks and shadows. Magic antiaging creams promised amazing results. She found herself lingering over one ad for a hair-smoothing serum made with black sesame seeds that promised to tame frizz and repair split ends.

She didn't get her hair trimmed nearly as often as she should, and when the humidity was bad, frizz could be a major problem.

There was a part of her that was always a little disgusted by makeup ads and the push to convince women they weren't good enough, no matter what they looked like. Another part of her wondered if she could pull off coral lipstick.

Her phone buzzed in her pocket. She lifted it and smiled at the name on the screen, pausing the TV before she swiped to answer. "Hey, baby. I was wondering when I'd hear from you."

"We're here in Lytle." Noah's voice was a balm. "It really lives up to its name. Population three thousand, and it seems like every single one of them speaks only Spanish."

"I thought you were learning Spanish with that little owl app on your phone."

He grunted. "On the bright side, the roach coach across the street from the hotel had fish tacos, so I'll probably have diarrhea later."

She laughed and shook her head. "Thanks for sharing."

"So you staying out of trouble?"

"Yes, of course."

"Of course, of course." She could hear his eye roll through the phone.

"I'll have you know I closed three cases today."

"That's excellent. Does that mean you've decided to let go of the Ballstow case?"

Winter bit her knuckle. "Does that sound like the sort of thing I would do?"

"Uh-oh."

"I just swung by the house this morning. Just for a quick look. And I saw the red."

"On what?"

She flicked another page in the catalog. Near the back were products other than cosmetics. Some jewelry, a bedazzled teddy bear, pillowcases made of Chinese silk. "It was in a trash bin on a brochure for JCH Bloom, that makeup line."

"Hmm. That seems like a very un-special thing to find, considering she was one of their representatives."

"I agree. I'm still trying to figure out what the heck I'm supposed to be looking at." She did a double take at the glitzy teddy bear. Did people really buy this crap?

"Maybe…you're supposed to treat yourself."

Winter put a hand on her hip. "Do you want me to spend money or make it? Make up your mind."

"I want you to do both. That's what money's for."

"I keep thinking about Nick."

"Who?"

"Nick Riley. The missing employee who was suing the literal pants off Brent Ballstow." She drummed her fingers on the glossy catalog in her lap. "But then I find this, and I wonder if maybe this catalog's trying to tell me the cops are focusing on the wrong person. Maybe this wasn't about Brent at all. Maybe it's about Lily."

"Trust your instincts. They've gotten you this far."

"Is that you giving me your blessing to keep digging into this?"

"Absolutely not."

She couldn't tell if he was joking.

"I wish I could be there with you." A hint of gravel entered Noah's voice. "I don't like you handling all this by yourself."

"I'm fine. You need to focus on what you're doing."

There was a brief rustle on his end of the line. "Speaking of which, Eve's poking at her watch. I need to get down to the briefing with the team."

"Okay. I'll talk to you tomorrow. I love you."

"Love you too." She heard the muffled sound of Eve's voice in the background before Noah hung up.

Winter felt a little guilty for not mentioning the phone call from Timothy Stewart's aunt, but there wasn't a reason to get Noah involved in that just yet. He always got a little weird when she mentioned Tim.

When they went in to rescue Autumn and her sister Sarah from the clutches of Adam Latham, Autumn's old boss, Timothy, disguised as a girl and left in hiding in Justin's absence, had lunged at Winter with a knife. Noah had shoved her aside, taking the blade full-on in the gut. His surgeries and extended hospital stay had saved his life but left a nasty scar—physically and emotionally.

Sometimes, Winter got the impression Noah didn't hold out a lot of hope for Tim. He had told her once—and only once—that Tim's story was so similar to what had happened to Justin. Kidnapped by a twisted killer. Tortured, traumatized, psychologically destroyed. It was exactly what Douglas Kilroy had done to Justin when he was little, and what Justin had done to Tim. Noah worried Tim was too far gone to be saved.

Justin had made the boy into his little protégé. By Noah's logic, there was no hope for him.

Winter had gotten very upset when Noah said that. She'd actually stormed out of the house and not spoken to her husband for the rest of the day. After everything she'd done to save the boy, the notion that she had delivered him into a fate worse than death grated on her like sandpaper being rubbed on her skin until she bled.

Noah had apologized and said he was wrong. He'd also

reminded Winter, as he often did, that she'd done everything she could for the boy. She needed to let it go.

That was like sandpaper too. What kind of a person could ever let such a thing go? No matter how much Noah or anybody else tried to convince her otherwise, she was responsible for the violence Tim endured. She needed to make sure he was safe and healthy. That he was being given every resource he needed to process his trauma.

She'd lost one little boy into the void. She'd be damned if she'd lose another.

Sighing, Winter flipped the catalog over and slapped it down on the tray next to her mostly empty bowl. There, on the back cover, scribbled in black ink over the advertisement for a perfume called Silver Mist, was a string of handwritten numbers. *39584.*

She stilled. This was what the red glow had been leading her to—these five numbers.

But what did they mean?

18

Noah followed Eve down to the lobby to meet up with the other agents on the team. Then they moved as a group into a private room to discuss their plans. Agent Ruiz—Noah knew him only by name—was leading the raid. He was a veteran agent in his late forties with gray eyes that had clearly seen more than their fair share of crazy things over the years.

"I just got off the phone with our informant who works at the gas station." Ruiz addressed the team, his Mexican accent painting every word with softly rolled *R*s. "The handoff is taking place tomorrow, right around noon."

"Why the hell would they be doing the handoff in broad daylight?" Noah asked.

"Because they're getting desperate." Ruiz grimaced. "Their operation's been busted wide open, and now they're like a store having a *going out of business* sale. They're trying to make what money they can from the stock they have before they cut ties here and set up shop somewhere else. This is our last chance to catch these assholes and put a stop to this."

As Ruiz started going over the details of what they could expect from the handoff and what each team member would be responsible for during the raid, Noah found himself struggling to focus. All he could think about was Winter.

She'd seen the red glow around a clue related to the Ballstow case, and he knew that meant she wasn't going to be backing off that one anytime soon. The clue being vague and confusing only made the situation worse. Winter would become obsessed with trying to figure out what it meant. Any hope he had of convincing her to stay away had gone out the window the moment she saw red.

He didn't pretend to understand his wife's powers. But he absolutely believed in them. For whatever reason—whether from the brain damage she suffered as a child or from an inherited gene—there was something incredibly special about Winter that helped her know things that could not be known. See things that could not be seen.

Her powers were often confusing and always seemed to lead her on wild-goose chases. Bizarre though the clues were, they invariably led Winter to whatever foul thing she was after.

"Dalton?"

Noah startled inwardly at the sound of his own name. He looked at Ruiz. "Yes?"

"You and Taggart will be in the back of the SWAT van. Garcia, you're driving."

"Yes, sir!" the youngish ex-Navy Seal shouted.

"After teams one and two are in position, Garcia will pull the van up. Dalton and Taggart will move the hostages into the van away from any gunfire and then get them the hell out of Dodge."

"You got it."

Ruiz turned to the other agent. "Pisetti, you'll be on team three."

Noah focused on Ruiz, trying to memorize the positions the other agents would be in and to listen closely to the rundown. But, once again, his brain wandered back to Winter.

His anxiety over his wife's safety had only ramped up since they'd moved to Austin. But his concern had nothing to do with the city. Pound for pound, Austin was a pretty safe place.

It was the change in her career that had him on edge. In the FBI, though she was frequently in danger, she always had someone she could call for backup. Now it seemed she was in the same amount of danger day in and day out, but with fewer rules to govern her behavior and no one to come to her aid when she inevitably got in over her head.

He trusted Winter more than any other living person on planet Earth. And going to unfamiliar places and dealing with potentially dangerous strangers was an important part of her job. But he just wanted to be by her side, making sure she was safe through it all.

Eve nudged him in the arm and motioned with the tip of her nose toward Ruiz, her eyes popping as if to say, *Are you kidding me?*

Noah smiled sheepishly and trained his gaze hard on the briefing agent. Still, he could barely hear a word.

This Ballstow case was one thing. The more he thought about it, Noah realized he wasn't worried about Winter poking her nose into that situation specifically. He was worried about her being out in the field, period.

After all, less than two weeks ago, Noah had discovered the person who'd set up cameras all around Winter's office and sent her threatening messages from a restricted number was actually a member of Justin's online fan club. These sick, twisted freaks saw Justin Black, infamous serial killer, as some kind of hero.

They spent their time in dark web chat rooms discussing the merits of his various atrocities and talking about his escape from prison as if it were the second coming of Christ. And since Justin was obsessed with Winter, they were obsessed with her too.

Would one of the freaks try to pick up where Justin left off? When Justin kidnapped Winter, Noah had felt like his own heart had been ripped from his chest. He couldn't bear the thought of such a thing happening again. If he lost Winter…

Carl Gardner—the man who'd set up the cameras—was dead, and his entire computer setup was in FBI custody, but Noah hadn't heard any news back from forensics yet. Given his upcoming off-duty status, he knew he wouldn't be hearing about it directly, but Eve had promised to keep him informed on that case…and only that case.

Until they knew who else was involved in Gardner's scheme and brought them all to justice, Winter wouldn't be safe.

Noah didn't bring this up because he didn't want to scare her. She seemed satisfied that Carl was gone, and Noah had found and dismantled all the spy cameras. But Noah couldn't be satisfied. He couldn't forget. A threat against his wife was worse than a threat against himself, and he fully intended to find every last soul involved and put them in their place.

That was part of the reason he needed a sabbatical. So he could focus on his own passion case. Just like Winter.

But first, there were loose ends left here that needed to be tied up. He pulled himself back to the room and Ruiz's instructions. Young girls were still being lured from their homes and kidnapped. Beaten, raped, psychologically manipulated, and sold to the highest bidder. This team had a chance here and now to put an end to all of it. To capture and punish those responsible.

Noah needed to focus, before he jeopardized the chance to bring these monsters to justice.

19

The next morning, after Winter had popped into the office to handle some housekeeping tasks—like making sure Ariel got paid—she decided to take a little walk. She tried to pretend, if only for her own benefit, that she wasn't actually going anywhere, but her feet soon led her ten blocks north to JCH Bloom's official business address and their one and only brick-and-mortar store.

JCH Bloom was written with a golden flourish across the front of the building, just like the logo emblazoned on the catalog and seemingly on all their products. The door was painted a hot pink, the walls a paler, pastel shade of the same color.

When Winter walked inside, a little golden bell over the door tinkled. A young woman was rearranging a display of scented candles at the center of the store, placing them on a low, round table. She smiled at Winter as she stepped inside.

"Welcome! Let me know if I can help you find anything."

Winter nodded politely as she started a slow circle around the perimeter of the room.

Unlike most stores, there didn't seem to be much in the

way of stock. For many of the products, there was only one bottle with a sticker on the side that read, *tester*. She tried out some hand lotion and sniffed a few perfume samples. When she found a bottle of the black sesame hair serum, she tested it on a discrete strand and decided she had to purchase it. But there wasn't a bottle for her to pick up and take to the register.

As she casually pursued the rest of the products, she checked the barcode and looked at the tags. The product numbers consisted of seven digits preceded by a letter, which meant the number she had found scribbled on the catalog—39584—wasn't one of those.

On the largest display near the front of the store were neatly arranged business cards and pamphlets, along with catalogs of the new spring collection. The most prominently displayed pamphlet was all about the exciting and lucrative opportunity to become a JCH sales partner.

Enrich the lives of women by improving their beauty on the outside and the inside! JCH Bloom provides an environment and structure where women can work for themselves and still have a supportive team at their side. Join JCH Bloom to live the Confident Life!

"Are you interested in becoming a Personal Beauty Consultant?"

No, definitely not.

"Maybe..." Winter smiled. "I've been thinking about it."

"I can definitely help you decide if this is the right opportunity for you." The woman smiled with her perfect red lipstick and shiny white teeth. She looked like she easily could've modeled for one of the catalogs. Her makeup was something out of a YouTube tutorial. There were so many colors on her face. The contouring alone...

She led Winter to a little alcove at the back of the store, where they sat down together on a pink leather couch. "I'm

Amy, by the way. Amy Powell. I've been a Bloom girl since the very beginning. Last month, I hit triple diamond for the fourth time."

Amy lightly brushed her square French tips over a line of broaches pinned to her pearl-colored jacket. Twelve tiny diamonds in total.

"Sam Drewitt." Winter recycled the alias she had adopted for going undercover at the mountaineering store. She'd gone to all the trouble to get a fake ID and everything made. No sense in wasting a perfectly good alias.

"Tell me a little more about your situation, Sam. What were you looking for today when you walked in here?"

Winter's gaze drifted over the store, taking it all in. The empty shelves, the fresh flowers, the comfortable seating. Crystal chandeliers. A small fridge with a clear door sat next to the register, bottles of spring water, both natural and sparkling, on display.

This wasn't a store. It was a trap.

The beautiful woman smiled prettily, looking rich and peaceful. Like she really had it together.

Winter crossed her legs and set her hands lightly on her knee. "Well, I've been looking for a part-time job. Something I could do from home. My husband had to take a sabbatical from work, and I really want to help him out with the money. Our son is still pretty young, though."

"How old is he?"

"He's ten. He's in school all day, of course. But I still want to make sure I'm there for him when he gets home."

"I'm the same way." She pressed a hand to her chest. "My daughters are eight and nine, so I totally get it. You want to be able to drop them off in the morning and talk to them about their day when they get home. Mine are always starving, too, so I have to have snacks ready. What's your son's name?"

"Tim." It came out before she could stop it, the name at the tip of her tongue.

The name going round and round in her head like a carousel. The name that always curled her tongue and conjured the taste of hot blood and the sound of cracking bones.

Winter forced her hand to her side and crushed it into a fist, trying to fight off the flashbacks threatening to overtake her.

Part of her felt like she should claim the boy as her own because she was the only person alive who could really understand what he'd been through. Another part of her didn't want to claim him for exactly the same reason.

"You okay?" Amy asked, her face soft and warm.

"I'm fine." Winter forced a smile that hurt her lips. "It's just, Tim's a very troubled boy. Today wasn't the easiest of days."

Amy's gentle gaze softened even further, pity pooling in her eyes. "Is he special needs?"

"You could say that."

"All the more reason your work needs to be flexible."

For the next hour, Winter found herself wrapped up in expertly crafted conversation.

First, Amy interviewed her. After coaxing out details about Winter's family and money situation and values, Amy started with the real questions. Have you ever thought of running your own business? Where would you like to see yourself in five years? What if I said you can own a business selling products that sell themselves with unlimited earning potential and the freedom to live the life you've always wanted?

Finally, Amy launched into a sales pitch that would topple even the most skeptical of tightwads. By the time she got around to telling Winter the price of membership and inventory, Winter was half convinced selling JCH Bloom really would be the solution to all her and Noah's money woes. Maybe he'd become a rep too.

"You're extremely lucky to have come in and joined up today." Amy's enthusiasm frothed off her like bubbles in a bathtub.

"Why is that?" Winter fought to match her energy.

"Because our founder, Jessica Huberth, is here in her office. And she always insists on meeting the new recruits. Most representatives have to wait until a formal get-together to meet her, but I'm going to take you up to her office so she can personally give you some tips to get your business off on the right foot."

This was the part where Winter was supposed to quiver with excitement. She did her best. How clever of Jessica Huberth to make herself seem like some kind of celebrity who was difficult to meet.

Lily Ballstow was Jessica's niece. As Winter followed Amy to a small golden elevator in the back that took them to the second floor, she wondered how JCH Bloom's founder had taken the news about her family member's gruesome death.

They paused in a luxe waiting room, and Amy went into the office first by herself before waving Winter inside.

The aesthetic of Jessica's quarters matched the rest of the store, but with a more muted and serious vibe. Vertical stripes of two soft shades of pink lined the walls, and the windows were dressed in sheer white curtains. Jessica sat behind a minimalistic glass desk with gold detailing.

She looked just like her picture. A pixie cut of perfectly disheveled deep-brown curls. Sensational makeup. She smiled pleasantly as Winter entered and stood from her desk to shake her hand.

Winter stumbled a little to make herself seem nervous. "Nice to meet you, Ms. Huberth. I'm Sam Drewitt."

"Welcome to the team, Sam. And everyone calls me Jessica." She squeezed Winter's hand before letting go. "We're like family here."

"It's so great to meet you." Winter was embarrassed at how easy it was to gush. "I'm really excited to join the team."

Jessica sat back down and spread her arms wide, steepling her fingers on her glass desktop. "Selling for JCH Bloom is not as easy as girls like Amy make it look. It takes a woman with a big heart who really cares about her clients. And especially here in the beginning phases, it takes dedication to learning and always striving to be the best version of yourself."

Winter kept her eyes wide, like she was sucking up every word she was saying. "Right."

"When my daughter first started here, she struggled. I didn't give her any special treatment, mind you. She was in exactly the same spot as you are now. There was a time she was almost ready to give up. But she trusted in the system and in the process. She believed in the products, and she believed in herself. Now Sybil's number three in overall earnings." The skin on Jessica's neck tightened. "Two. She's number two. We lost one of our top earners recently."

It didn't take a detective to figure out she was talking about Lily Ballstow. Unfortunately, with all of Jessica's makeup and her clearly Botoxed brows and plumped-up lips, it was impossible to tell if she was sad about that.

Jessica smiled. "Amy told me you signed up for our Silver Tier, is that right?"

Winter nodded. The Silver Tier was four hundred fifty dollars and included a large array of cosmetics and other products for her to sell, as well as the company's educational materials.

She put the whole thing on her business credit card. This

was business, technically. A pro bono case. Lawyers did it, so why not private investigators?

She certainly wasn't trying to hide the expense from her husband, and she fully intended to tell Noah all about it when she saw him next. But she was a grown woman, and they trusted each other to make decisions like this without a roundtable discussion preceding every one of them.

Hopefully, by the time she talked with Noah, she'd have something to show for it—evidence that was worth four hundred fifty dollars and then some.

"I'm going to give you the same advice I gave my daughter when she started out." Jessica sat straight in her chair, folding her hands in her lap. Though she was only about five feet tall, she exuded the energy of a colossus. "No doesn't mean no. No—"

"Means not yet!"

Winter turned at the sound of this new voice to see a younger version of Jessica Huberth strut in.

"Sybil! Speak of the devil."

"Mother, I'm in and out, just grabbing a shipment, but Amy said there was a new recruit." Sybil turned to Winter, hand out. "Hi! I'm Sybil Huberth, it's amazing to meet you…"

"Sam Drewitt."

"Well, Sam, welcome. Wow, you're so pretty. Isn't she so pretty, Mom?"

"She is."

Sybil stepped back and unabashedly appraised Winter's face. "Can you imagine her with some of our new cream rouge and lip tint?"

"I can."

"And I'd love to get my hands on those eyes and smoke 'em right up!" She clapped her hands together.

For a second, Winter thought Sybil was going to grab her

by the chin and start painting. Fortunately, the spitfire seemed to recall she was on a tight schedule.

"Oh, anyway, gotta run. Toodles!" With a smile that lit up her face, nearly making her eyes disappear, she added, "But you're going to be great." She spun on a strappy designer heel and was gone.

Sybil's charismatic attitude was on full display across her features as she waved goodbye and left. As exhausting as that whirlwind introduction and exit had been, it was interesting to see what Jessica used to look like in her younger days, before all the facework. Especially the visibility of some emotion.

Winter turned back to Jessica. "She's really enthusiastic. It must be wonderful to work together, mother and daughter."

Jessica pursed her lips. "It has its moments."

Winter laughed but wondered what that meant. Did Sybil have an off button? And, if so, was Jessica referring to a dark side?

"Now, where were we?" Jessica smiled, which stretched her face right out. It looked painful. "Oh, yes, all refusals are simply requests for more information. Trust me, once you get even one JCH Bloom product in a customer's hand, you will have created a lifelong relationship that will be fulfilling for them and lucrative for you."

The door opened, and Amy came sashaying back into the room, a pink bag with the JCH logo in her arms. "For you. And we tossed in our new lip tint that Sybil picked out special on her way out."

"Thank you." Winter plastered on a smile. These women sure got excited about lotions, potions, glosses, and creams. When was the last time she was that excited about something so…arbitrary?

"Congratulations on making the best choice for your family and your future." Jessica spoke without irony, as though she genuinely believed her own vacuous sentiments. "Now get out there and sell your cute little butt off."

Winter inwardly sneered but held her forced smile anyway. After all, she hadn't actually come here to work.

A moment later, Amy reappeared with a flourish of free samples. Winter said goodbye to Jessica and let Amy usher her out the door with a volley of clichés, back into the real world.

20

Back at the office, Winter told Ariel all about her new side gig as a JCH Bloom girl, which made her assistant laugh so much that coffee came out her nose. Making themselves cozy in the little seating area Kline had set up near the bookshelves, the two of them dumped the contents of the sample bag out on the oval coffee table.

A pamphlet inside explained that this was her sales bag—what she would carry with her to let clients test products before purchase. Her actual inventory would be shipped to the office in the next few days. They found tiny tubes of lipstick, individual mascara wands, cotton swabs, and the just-for-her lip tint.

Winter tried out the coral lipstick and checked herself in the compact with a flip-up mirror that housed some powder. Her cool white skin, icy-blue eyes, and pitch-black hair clashed hard with the warm color. "I look like a clown."

Ariel giggled some more, which made Winter laugh.

"OMG, smell this." Ariel held out a scratch-and-sniff perfume sample card.

Winter leaned in and took a whiff. "Mmm. Smells like chocolate chip cookies."

"I want to smell like a chocolate chip cookie." Ariel rubbed the card on her collar bone.

"Well, I can hook you up with a bottle. I'm pretty sure it comes with my inventory."

"You're not actually planning on selling any of the stuff you ordered?"

Winter sat back in her chair, which was identical to the one Ariel sat in. They were both very modern looking—white leather and shaped vaguely like angular bananas with no armrests. And shockingly comfortable.

"I might if the case calls for it, but probably not. I guess I kinda just bought four hundred and fifty dollars' worth of cosmetics for personal use."

"I do that literally every time I walk up to a makeup counter. Don't beat yourself up."

Winter was amazed to discover that Ariel's confession made her feel a little better. "Thanks." She wiped off the coral lipstick and picked up the lip tint called Orchid. It was glossy, translucent. It felt warm and gooey going on.

"So did you find anything out? And that color looks amazing."

Pouting her pretty magenta lips into the compact, Winter sank deeper into her albino banana. "I didn't discover much. I mean, the business seems a little shady, but no more so than any other pyramid scheme. The founder of the company, Jessica Huberth, was Lily's aunt. But I just don't see how Lily's side business selling makeup could have anything to do with her murder."

"I'll keep digging into the company. See if I can pull anything up."

"Thanks." Winter picked up something called Brilliant

Diamonds Sensational Sparkles Eye Cream and smeared the tip of one finger with glitter.

"That woman called again this morning. Suzannah Hall-Tolle. She asked for your cell number and took 'umbrage' when I refused to give it to her."

"She took umbrage?"

"Her words, obvs." Ariel opened a little plastic case of furry eyelashes. "I looked her up online and didn't find much. She's a widow, no kids, seems to have lots of money. Her social media feeds are nothing but Bible quotes and reposts of articles from *The Federalist*."

"Fantastic work." Winter had to throw herself forward to get out of the chair, which was trying to lull her into taking a nap. "I think I'm going to have to leave you on your own this afternoon."

"Why? Where are you going this time?"

"I need to go to San Antonio and check on something."

"Noah?"

Winter wrinkled her nose. "He's not in San Antonio. He's in someplace called Lytle."

"Lytle is right by San Antonio. Like a half an hour from downtown, tops."

"Really?" Her heart brightened. After promising Suzannah that she'd look into Tim's welfare, a phone call seemed painfully insufficient. Really, Winter wanted to check on Tim for her own sake, to honor the dreams she kept having about him and to make sure he was okay. It was a prospect she'd been low-key dreading ever since speaking to Suzannah. Knowing she'd also be able to drop in and surprise Noah made the whole thing more bearable.

Still, her stomach was twisted in knots. She'd told Noah only about her initial dream of Tim, not the subsequent dreams. And she'd very purposefully not mentioned the call from Suzannah.

Keeping anything from him was like swallowing a handful of nails, but knowing she'd be able to pop in on him soothed some of that pain. She knew how happy he'd be to see her. They could hang out in his cheap motel room together and have sex on the squeaky bed. Just like the olden days when they worked together. And she'd have a chance to tell him the truth about Tim, Suzannah, and her continuing nightmares.

"I'm gonna head out now." Winter started toward her office to pack up her computer. "Please, give me a call if you find anything about JCH Bloom that stands out to you."

"You got it, Boss." Ariel batted the comically huge fake lashes she'd just put on. "When will you be back?"

"I'll see you tomorrow morning." When she stepped up to the door that separated her little office from the rest of the space, Winter paused and turned back. "If you'd rather work from home this afternoon, that's totally fine with me."

Ariel smiled, though it looked like a frown. "Thanks."

Winter gathered up her things and headed out the door.

The drive to San Antonio would take about an hour and a half, and she had to run home first to pack an overnight bag. She wanted to get to Guy Hall's house to check things out before Tim would be home from school. She didn't want to have to actually see the boy, to look into his golden-brown eyes and remember the way he screamed as he watched his parents and sister die…as Justin's gleeful laughter echoed all around them like a curse.

Though Winter wanted to do everything she could to help Tim and make sure he was safe and cared for, she didn't want to be around him. The memories were too painful.

21

Winter had Guy's address pulled up on her phone. He lived in Hill Country Village, about fifteen miles out from downtown San Antonio. It seemed to be an exclusive neighborhood for those who wanted to be close to the city but without the hustle and bustle.

Tim attended the local school, Hidden Forest Elementary, a few miles away from the house. That was where Winter headed first.

Pulling up to the school, Winter parked under the shade of some trees with trunks with white bark like aspens, only thicker. Slabs of white and red concrete led up to the front doors of the square gray building. A big banner out front proclaimed the name of the school along with a picture of their mascot—some kind of bird of prey.

The recess bell rang, clanging exactly like every school bell since the dawn of time. Wild children burst from the doors and swarmed the playground equipment. Others got out on the field with a soccer ball and seemed to pick up where their last game left off.

She'd told herself she didn't want to see him, that she'd

come to check on the house at exactly this time so she wouldn't have to make visual contact, but her heart had led her astray once again. She didn't want him to see her, though.

She scanned the playground, searching for a little boy with floppy golden-brown hair. Tim was a little tall for his age and skinny, his body composed mostly of two long legs. She knew that recesses were staggered so all the grades weren't let out at once. That would be chaos. Still, she let her gaze skip from child to child, playing an anxious game of Where's Waldo.

A boy stepped out the doors behind all the others. His hair had been buzzed short, and he had a tan going, but Winter still recognized him instantly. Tim kept his face turned to the ground, with his hands shoved deep inside the pockets of his khaki shorts—the school uniform.

A dodgeball came flying at his head. He flinched and dived out of the way, so the ball struck the brick behind him. The child who kicked the ball laughed, and he and his friends pointed, shouting something she could only assume was cruel.

Tim ignored them and kept walking. Past the playground equipment, past the field, past the tables where groups of girls sat huddled around notebooks. He walked to a utility shed at the far edge of the lot and sat down behind it, alone and out of sight.

Winter's heart cracked open. Gently, she eased her Honda forward so she could get a look at the boy. He had a book in his hands, and his nose was buried between the covers, legs drawn up tight to his chest.

Suddenly, she was consumed by the intense urge to know what he was reading. Winter took out the small binoculars she always kept in the glove compartment and peered through them.

James and the Giant Peach. The story of an orphan boy whose parents were killed and who ended up the ward of two wicked aunts who beat him and treated him like a slave, until one day, magic allowed him to escape by sailing across the world in a piece of massive fruit, accompanied by a ragtag group of giant insects.

Winter sighed and gripped a fistful of fabric on her shirt, over the spot where her heart sat breaking in her chest. Part of her wanted to go talk to him. She seriously considered it. But when Tim glanced up, she instinctively ducked down to be sure he wouldn't see her.

"You're being ridiculous," Winter chastised herself, but she didn't sit up. She started the engine and pulled away from the school, leaving Tim to his literary isolation.

Only when she was a good block away from the school did she sit fully erect in her seat and shake off the invisible ants crawling around inside her clothes. Her mind swirled as memories of trauma flashed through her senses. No words, just feelings and sounds.

She finally had to pull over and take a few deep breaths, letting the flashback wash over her. Her fingers gripped the steering wheel, and her eyes clenched themselves shut. For a horrible moment, she felt like she was back in that trailer with Justin and Tim's family. Justin had pressed the gun against his sister's head and ordered Winter to kill his parents. If she refused, he would shoot both of them and then kill Tim too.

The crack of bone under her fingers. The sound of death ringing in her ears. Winter clenched her fists and tried to remember how to breathe.

She couldn't have said how long she sat on the side of the road, waiting for the pain and sensations to subside, but eventually, they did. In her extensive research on the workings of PTSD and how it affected—and would continue to affect—her for the rest of her life, Winter had learned that during a flashback, the verbal center of the brain shut down.

That was why, at times, all she could remember were feelings and sensations. She had to activate her parasympathetic nervous system to escape. And the best way to do that was to exhale very, very slowly.

When Winter came back to herself, she loaded Guy Hall's address onto her phone again and followed the directions. It was helpful to give herself something menial to focus on, like driving. By the time she pulled up to the massive house nestled in the forest, her heartbeat had nearly returned to normal.

Guy's house was attractive but not ostentatious. At the end of a cul-de-sac, the property had a generous, fenced-in lawn with a garden. The house was more modest than the others in the neighborhood, though Guy could have afforded something much bigger. Apparently, the man preferred a less conspicuous lifestyle.

Winter didn't pull all the way up to the house. Instead, she parked at the side of the long driveway and walked the rest of the way. The trees above her burst with tiny white flowers, harbingers of spring. The floral smell rushed into her lungs and soothed her instantly, mainly because it didn't remind her of anything.

She noticed a three-car garage off to one side, the doors closed. The house seemed still and empty. Winter walked up to the front door, rang the bell, and stepped back and waited. And waited.

Nobody was home. That fact sent a wave of relief washing over her, followed by a tiny pinch of guilt. The truth was, she had no idea what she was going to say to Tim's uncle if he had answered.

"Sorry to bug you on a Wednesday, but I'm the woman who killed your sister. I'm here because your other sister thinks you're a

drunk who's unfit to take care of a child. Is there any truth to that?"

"Thank God he's not home."

She stepped down from the porch and took a few cautious steps toward the front window before leaning over the hedge to peer inside.

The house had vaulted ceilings with exposed runners, honey-colored hardwood floors, and not much else. Sparse furniture, no rugs. No toys or backpacks or random shoes scattered about the floor. The living room had only one armchair and a coffee table. No books. No television. It looked like a show home, not someplace where people actually lived, let alone a child.

But this was just one room. It wasn't unheard of for some rooms to be sectioned off only for adults. For all Winter knew, there could be a gorgeous playroom upstairs or in the basement. All she'd really learned was that Tim's uncle embraced minimalism. Hardly damning evidence of a neglectful drunk.

Winter looked around for garbage cans, hoping to dive in and search for empty bottles, but they must've been locked away somewhere out of sight.

The longer she lingered, the more out of place she felt. For the life of her, she couldn't remember why she'd come or what she'd hoped to gain.

With a heavy heart, she returned to her vehicle and left the property.

22

Winter cuddled deeper into her husband's shoulder, the postcoital haze slowly fading from her brain. To say he'd been excited when she randomly showed up at his motel was a massive understatement.

Sunlight glowed beyond thick curtains, the afternoon warming the room. The smell of sweat was in the curtains and in the sheets. Winter started to wonder how many people had had sex in this bed before them. Deciding that was not a helpful line of inquiry, she shoved the thought away.

"I missed you." Noah squeezed her tighter, his heavy hand on the small of her back. He kissed her hair, her temple. "I'm so glad you came."

Winter laughed, fuzzy little bubbles popping pleasantly in her stomach. "I missed you too. I don't like sleeping alone."

"Me either. I need to feel your butt against me every night or I can't sleep."

"I can stay the night, but I'll have to get up early. I promised Ariel I'd be in the office tomorrow morning."

"No. I'm not letting you go." He squeezed her again. "I can't believe you came to see me."

"Well, I had to go to San Antonio, and when I saw you were so close, I figured I could turn it into an overnight."

"Lucky me." Noah touched her chin and encouraged her to look at him so he could kiss her lips. "So what's the new case?"

"Uh..." Winter's lips thinned. "Tim Stewart."

The seize in Noah's muscles was subtle but there. Every part of his body from his forehead to his toes tightened. "What about him?"

How could she answer that without ruining his up-until-now wonderful mood?

"There's a custody thing going on with his uncle and his aunt. I need to make sure he ends up with whichever one will give him the best chance."

Noah groaned, and he rolled onto his back and tucked a hand behind his neck. He closed his eyes. "At least it's not about the friggin' Ballstows."

Winter bit her lip. "About that..."

"What?" One of his eyes opened and peered at her.

"Don't get mad." Winter leaned over his bare chest and fiddled with the USMC dog tags he wore around his neck. She didn't know why she ever bothered trying to keep anything from Noah. The best-laid plans would fall to pieces the moment she looked at him and blurted out everything.

"I signed up to be a representative for JCH Bloom."

"I have no idea what that means."

"You know, the cosmetics company. From the catalog I told you about."

Noah settled deeper into the mattress and shifted to look at her. "Okay. Tell me about it."

After explaining about the glowing red numbers she'd

found written in pen on the back of the catalog, Winter confessed about the money she had spent buying into an MLM cosmetics company. She figured that was a fight a lot of wives had had with their husbands over the years, but at least she had a compelling ulterior motive.

"I don't really have a plan. At this point, I just need to figure out what those numbers mean. And I know they have something to do with JCH Bloom. I'm not so sure that what happened to the Ballstows has anything to do with Brent or his business."

"It could be a coincidence. Maybe the numbers are totally unrelated, and the catalog is just what 'whoever' happened to write them on."

That was an irritatingly good point. But there was no profit in that line of thinking, so she might as well stay the current course. "I'm sorry about the money. I just went down to the shop to check the place out, but then the lady started talking so fast. Becoming a part of the company is the best way to find out what's really going on down there. The best way to find out about the numbers."

"Well…" Noah took a deep groan of an inhale. "I'm not exactly thrilled, but I'm not surprised either."

Winter smacked his chest lightly. "What's that supposed to mean?"

"The moment you found a glowing red clue, I knew any hope of pulling you off this thing was out the window." He absently stroked her hair. "When I'm with you is the only time I feel all right."

Winter watched his face, the subtle twitch of his closed eyelids. "How's the job going here?"

"It hasn't really started yet." He grimaced, and turned his head to gaze straight up to the ceiling. "I think I've lost my touch."

She wiggled closer to him. "I can attest that that's not true."

"No, I'm serious. I can't seem to focus on a damn thing. I really do think it's time you and me got away from all this for a while. I looked up this little resort in Oahu. It's gorgeous there."

It was the second time in two conversations Noah had mentioned vacation. The first time, she'd kind of brushed it off as a joke.

"Why can't you focus? What are you thinking about instead?"

"You." He sat up, knees bent in front of him. "I can't stop obsessively worrying about you. Every time you're out of my sight, I can't help worrying it'll be the last time I ever see you."

Her heart melted, and Winter grabbed onto his arm. "You don't need to worry about me. I'm okay. I'm tough as nails."

"I wish I could stop. I want to stop."

An almost imperceptible quaver in his voice told her what he was really saying. "Is this about when I was kidnapped?"

Noah tightened his teeth. "What would you think about working together again? You and me, side by side."

"That would be the dream."

"'Cause if you'd rather I didn't come work with you at the agency, I could always start my own bounty-hunting business instead."

"Hold up. Why the hell wouldn't I want you? Of course I want you!" Winter punched him in the arm. "Idiot."

He smiled and nodded along. She waited for him to speak, but he didn't.

"So this sabbatical of yours… Is it just temporary, or would you really leave the FBI permanently?"

He slid back down next to her and gathered her into his arms. "I don't know."

"I want you to do whatever you want to do." She snuggled deep into his side. "Whatever will make you happy. I would love to add you permanently to the team whenever you're ready."

23

Noah waited near the SWAT van, which was parked behind a low billboard across the street from the gas station. Eve stood at his side, the hood of her black plastic poncho up to shield her eyes.

The sky crackled with pale-yellow lightning, a steady drizzle soaking the town below. The dirt parking lot had degraded into a mud patch, but the air was fresh and sweet. The bluebonnets were in bloom all around. Usually, he would've said they had no smell at all, but today, he could taste them like honey on his tongue.

If their informant was to be trusted, and Ruiz insisted that he was, the handoff was scheduled to take place any minute now. When Ruiz gave the signal, the van would get into position up against the vehicle holding the hostages, and Noah and Eve would help them to safety, securing them in the armored vehicle.

Every agent on the scene was dressed in full gear. Fatigues, helmets, bulletproof vests. Noah's primary weapon —an HK MP5 submachine gun with a collapsible stock—was in his hands. A subload pistol was holstered securely at his hip.

Last time Noah had come up against these guys, shots had been fired almost immediately. There was every reason to expect today would be the same. If they didn't know several innocent people faced a fate worse than death if they didn't intervene here and now, they would've looked for a lower-risk scenario.

Sometimes, that simply isn't an option.

Noah felt cool and relaxed and focused for the first time in weeks. He was ready for anything. In the Marines, he discovered he had a kind of action mode. A place he could get into mentally where his problems and even his personality fell away enough that he could maintain laser-like focus on the present. It had kept him alive in combat more times than he could possibly count and served him well through all his years with the FBI.

The threat of immediate danger had never bothered him. Not in the moment anyway. There was a storage bin in the back of his mind where he could stuff all his fear, trauma, and emotions so they wouldn't get in the way. Sometime later—he never could predict just when, though it was always at a quiet and safe time—the bin would fly open, and he'd have to deal with whatever he'd shoved in there.

But ever since Justin kidnapped Winter, this system had grown weaker, and at times, it collapsed completely. Maybe Falkner had sensed that in him. His focus hadn't been on the job, and lately, he'd lost his ability to live in the present. So often he found his attention wandering to the past or the future. Worry, anxiety, worry, anxiety. The constant ebb and flow of things he could not control was holding him hostage most days.

Control rested in the present. Combat was in the present.

Today, Noah would prove to himself that he hadn't lost his touch.

Deep breaths. Visualize the situation. Trust your muscles and your instincts. They know what to do.

A wink of chrome coming down the road captured Noah's attention. An oversize black van with darkened windows moved gradually, maintaining the speed limit and coming to a full stop at the yield sign before pulling into the muddy lot behind the gas station.

Ruiz spoke through the radio that buzzed in Noah's ear, alerting the team.

Eve's shoulder brushed Noah's as she stepped up beside him and peered through binoculars at the van. "Looks like it could be our guy."

Noah nodded. The windows were darkened so no one could see inside. The van passed by them before parking under an overhanging tree, just beyond their sight.

A moment later, a white delivery truck came toward the gas station from the other direction. It moved slowly and parked right out front by the pumps.

A greasy-looking man in a white Cowboys baseball cap stepped out from the white delivery truck and went into the gas station. He was inside for a few minutes, chatting with the undercover agent who'd been working the counter for the last three weeks, ever since the owner of the gas station was arrested for his part in the trafficking ring.

Cowboys Ball Cap emerged with a pack of cigarettes in one hand and an energy drink in the other. He looked to be in his late thirties or early forties, skinny and tall with sunken cheeks. Noah noticed a slight bulge in the back of his pants—a gun tucked in his belt.

He lit a cigarette, his head slinging back and forth as he checked for danger. Noah had to smirk. There were five vehicles on his perimeter and twelve federal agents watching his every move, and yet this bozo felt perfectly secure with his once-over.

Cowboys Ball Cap was experiencing his last moments of freedom for what Noah hoped would be a very, very long time. Was he aware of that on any level? Would he act differently if he were? Noah decided he wouldn't. He was just another dumb, arrogant criminal. The man didn't even bother to pretend to be getting gas.

He cupped the cigarette under his palm to protect it from the rain and kept his head down as he headed back to his truck, where he stood by the driver's side door, looking impatient as he side-eyed the van. After a while, he lit another cigarette.

Eve pressed in a little closer, peering over Noah's shoulder through her own binoculars. "What the hell is he waiting for?"

Noah swept his gaze toward where he knew the van was parked, then back to Cowboys Ball Cap standing by the truck. "He must be the buyer. He's waiting for the seller to make a move."

"Maybe this is his first time, then."

Noah nodded. "If their regular buyers know we've been cracking down on the ring, they might've backed off. It goes with the whole theory that they're just unloading what they've got left before cutting ties to start the business up somewhere else."

"I don't think that's gonna work out for them."

The radio cut into their conversation, Ruiz's voice quick and sharp. "The driver is exiting the van."

A moment later, a man in a straw hat approached the smoker by the truck. He was short and squat with a large mustache—an honest, down-home, workaday-looking kind of guy. The sort who always had dirt under his fingernails. Usually, men who looked like him were at least somewhat trustworthy, or so went the stereotype. Nine times out of ten, they were at least predictable.

Just goes to show you should never judge a book by its cover.

Straw Hat stepped up to Cowboys Ball Cap. They shook hands and began to speak. This was the transaction part. Overall, the exchange seemed friendly and polite. At one point, the lanky cigarette guy got out his phone and stood shoulder to shoulder with the squat gardener type as they both looked at the screen. Maybe he was sending the money now on some dark web banking server.

It was irritating how technologically advanced even low-level criminals were getting. Noah often wished he lived in the days when they just handed each other suitcases full of cash or when bank robbers proudly announced themselves by name as they burst through the doors, tommy guns in hand.

Those were the days.

Watching their gestures, Noah could guess what they were saying. Straw Hat was telling Cowboys Ball Cap to pull his truck up behind the van so they could open the two back doors and shuffle the terrified hostages between them. Nobody would see and nobody would be the wiser. The women and children would disappear into a network of forced labor and sexual servitude for the rest of their short lives, as so many had all over the world.

Today, a few souls would be given another chance. There was no doubt that whoever was locked in that van had already been subjected to horrible things. Noah couldn't change that. All he and any of the other agents could do was change what happened from this moment forward.

Noah's heart beat steady and strong. He tightened his muscles, held himself taut, and let his body relax into readiness.

"We can confirm at least two more men in the van and

one additional man in the truck." Ruiz's voice carried clearly into their ears. "Wait for the truck to get into position."

Twelve agents encircled the gas station, every one of them armed. But it was necessary to assume all five men on the scene were armed as well, and there might yet be more armed men in the back of the van with the hostages—keeping them quiet and under control.

Cowboys Ball Cap flicked his cigarette. The orange tip pinwheeled against the gray, overcast sky. With one last handshake, he got into his truck, slowly pulled out of the gas station, and headed across the street toward the van, passing the other man as he walked back to his vehicle.

Noah and Eve climbed into the back of the SWAT van.

A moment later, Ruiz began calling units to move in. Teams one and three moved first to flank the vehicles and secure the route, and then the SWAT van moved into position.

The van parked, and Noah threw open the doors. He and Eve rushed out into the heavy rain. He registered Cowboys Ball Cap to his left getting thrust face-first against the side of his truck, an agent cuffing him and checking him for weapons.

"FBI! Hands in the air!" another agent shouted as he ripped open the truck door and forced out the man in the back seat.

A shot fired, and Noah's head snapped back to the van. Someone in the passenger seat was firing out the window—a semiautomatic by the sound of it. The team returned fire with their machine guns in quick controlled bursts, peppering the metal door and shattering glass.

Noah didn't stop to watch. He needed to get the hostages out of the van and into the bulletproof SWAT vehicle before any more shots were fired.

"Cover me!" He rushed forward, keeping his head down

and his shoulders up. Another burst of shouting and gunfire cut the air as Noah wrenched open the van's back door.

The smell hit him before his eyes could process the scene. Piss and vomit and sweat—unwashed and huddled humanity. Against the freshness of rain and the sweetness of bluebonnets, the stench was even more nauseating, a shock to the senses like a punch in the face.

About two dozen individuals were packed in the back, pressed together like sardines in a tin. Around half were young women and the rest were children, both boys and girls. Most of them had dark eyes and dark hair and looked vaguely Latine. Their hands were zip-tied together, their clothes scant and filthy, and all appeared to be barefoot. Many hid their eyes and retreated into themselves, collectively pulling back from the light and chaos.

Noah blinked as a man stood up from the huddled group. Clean clothes, a heavy jacket. He raised his arm.

"FBI! Drop it!"

The man didn't stop. Noah tapped the trigger and three bullets slammed into the man's chest, knocking him back. His arms flew up, and he dropped the pistol.

The women and children screamed, covered their heads with their cuffed arms, and pressed themselves into the floor of the van. Under normal circumstances, he might've expected people caught in gunfire to scatter like roaches in a kitchen light, but not one of them tried to make a break for it. Like dogs living their whole lives trapped in a cage, it didn't occur to them to run.

He rushed over to the pistol and picked it up before sweeping his gaze over the man. Three identical wounds bloomed like red roses on his chest, but he was still breathing.

"Medic! We got a man down!" Noah glanced around for

Eve. She stood with her back to him, facing outward with her gun raised. She spoke into her radio.

Noah turned back to the frightened hostages. "It's okay. You're safe now. *Ven conmigo*. Come with me."

It took a moment for them to realize what was going on. But when they did, the women moved first and helped usher the children into the back of the SWAT van, which had been stocked with medical supplies, water, and blankets. Two SWAT medics cut their ties and began tending them, and Noah moved out to help assess the damage and secure the perimeter.

An ambulance rushed away to Medina Regional Hospital in San Antonio, ferrying the man Noah shot, along with one other trafficker. Soon, more would follow with the less critically injured—especially those poor souls they'd come here to rescue from such inhumane conditions.

Agent Ruiz ended up with a ricochet wound in his right thigh that required dressing on the scene, but no other LEOs and no hostages were wounded in the skirmish. Altogether, six traffickers were arrested, and eighteen hostages were taken into FBI protective custody.

The job was done. With a little luck and a lot of maneuvering, they would be able to get at least one of the traffickers to crack under pressure and tell them if any more women and children were being held against their will. They might even get the names of more of the ring's regular buyers and rescue some of the victims who'd already changed hands before bringing an end to the trafficking ring once and for all.

Once the scene was secured and all parties had been handed off to other authorities and escorted to their appropriate destinations, Ruiz led an informal AAR where the agents discussed everything that had gone down.

Noah felt his anxiety and worry slowly but surely settle

back into place. During the action, he'd enjoyed the short respite from himself, but now all he could do was think how much it sucked that he was going to have to hang around Lytle for the next few days to help clear away all the red tape left over from this little excursion.

He wanted to be with Winter, to make sure she was staying safe.

Back at the hotel, Noah took the opportunity to call his wife. He knew she wanted to be kept in the loop about the raid. Besides that, he had a niggling pain in his stomach, a warning that something was wrong. Of course, red beacons weren't directing his attention this way or that. All he had were memories of things gone wrong to help him navigate the future.

The phone rang and rang before eventually going to voicemail. He called again and got more of the same. The pain in his gut intensified, urging him to go home and check on her.

Noah took a deep breath and told himself she was fine. There was nothing to worry about. The sooner he got this case processed and tied up, the sooner his sabbatical could begin.

At last, he would be able to stay at her side.

24

Having failed to get up early, twice, Winter didn't get back to Austin and into work until one o'clock.

When she stepped in, her back achy from the ride, Ariel was already there waiting for her.

"Good afternoon!" Ariel hopped up from her desk. She was wearing a lot more makeup than usual—fake lashes, cat eyes, contour. Winter could only assume she'd been playing around with the Bloom bag. "Perfect timing."

Winter slid her jacket off and hung it on the hook by the door. "What do you mean?"

"Miss Jessica Huberth is not as sparkling clean as she seems."

"Please don't tell me this is an April Fool's joke." She took a seat in the chair near Ariel's desk.

Ariel grinned. "Nope, but there might be a whoopee cushion or two around the place."

Winter groaned. "Great." She tapped Ariel's desk. "As much as I'd prefer to talk about farts instead of murders, we'd better focus."

"Spoilsport." Ariel winked before turning serious. "Jessica

Huberth divorced a felon about three years ago. Kyle Fobb. He'd gotten arrested and served over a year in prison for dealing drugs, and it was during that time that she served him papers." Ariel pulled up his image on her tablet. "But before all that, she filed the articles of incorporation for JCH Bloom."

"Really?"

Winter and Ariel studied Kyle Fobb's mug shot. He wasn't unattractive.

"And that wasn't his first stint. He's been in and out of prison since he became an adult."

"All drug-related?"

"No. In his early twenties, he did three years for a B and E. A homeowner caught him in the act, and he beat her unconscious."

"Any domestic violence charges with Jessica?"

Ariel shook her head. "Not that I could find."

"Is she still in contact with him?"

"I didn't proof that she was. Except that when she was starting her business, she got nearly all the initial capital to the tune of seven figures from a woman named Colleen Sturgis."

"Okay?" Winter tilted her head, waiting for Ariel to make the connection.

"Colleen Sturgis was a longtime friend of Jessica's ex-husband. They were neighbors growing up. And about a decade ago, she spent six months at a rehab facility for opioid addiction." She tapped her screen. "It's pretty easy to tell from her social media she's relapsed since then."

"So Fobb connected his ex-wife Jessica with Sturgis to get the company up and running before going to prison on felony drug charges." Winter drummed her fingers on her thigh. "And you think Colleen Sturgis was one of Kyle Fobb's clients before he went to prison, and she is again right now? As in, he's dealing again?"

"That's my hunch. She'd likely contact her old dealers for supply if she started using again, and he's been out for two years." Ariel smiled smugly.

"Good work, Ariel. Very good work. We'll make a P.I. out of you yet."

"I found the most recent contact information for both of them too. It's in your email."

"What did I ever do without you?"

Her face warmed gently. "Aw, thanks. That means a lot to me."

Winter flashed a quick smile before returning to the hook by the door to throw her jacket back on. "I think I'm gonna go have a word with Jessica Huberth's silent partner, Colleen Sturgis. They probably just happened to meet through Jessica's ex-husband back when they were still married, though, and there won't be anything remotely interesting to find. That's the kind of luck I've been having lately."

"Your luck will change soon. It always does."

On her way out the door, Winter noticed a letter sitting atop the mail pile. Larger than a standard envelope, it had perforated edges designed to be stripped away, and the sender was Cumberland Mountain Climbing Equipment. Winter had recently gone undercover as an employee at the sporting goods store, though she'd only worked a few shifts before blowing her cover.

Opening the envelope, she found the answer to one of her problems…a paycheck.

25

Winter double-checked the address was right as she pulled up to Colleen Sturgis's mansion. An ambulance was out front, lights flashing, along with a fire engine and no less than three police cars. Someone had put up yellow tape around the perimeter of the home, and lookie-loos were milling about.

She parked across the street. After stepping out, she took a moment to survey the scene. Her gaze was immediately drawn to Detective Darnell Davenport, who seemed to be the one in charge.

Homicide was there. A stone dropped in Winter's stomach as she started forward. That did not bode well for Colleen Sturgis.

She knew Darnell wouldn't be happy to see her. Of course, regardless of any social unpleasantness she might experience, Winter had to know what happened.

Noah was right about that. The second she saw that red glow on Lily Ballstow's JCH Bloom catalog, there was no turning back.

"Darnell!" Winter called, waving to him from the other

side of the tape. He tipped his head up, eyes hidden behind big sunglasses. Winter saw the furrow in his brow, though. The wrinkle that clearly demanded, *What the hell are you doing here?*

He gave her a curt upward nod. After speaking with a few more techs and uniforms, he made his way over.

"Are you stalking me?" Darnell cocked his chin, the sunlight glinting off his shades.

"Hardy har." She looked him up and down, assessing the recent changes in his appearance. The goatee transformed his face. She might not have even recognized him if she hadn't seen him in proper context, wearing that same suit he always wore. "You look like Damon Wayans."

"Gee. Is that what you came here to tell me?" He took off his sunglasses in a meaningful way. "What's up?"

"I came to talk to Colleen Sturgis."

"You're a little late. She was murdered."

Every vague thing Winter had been wondering about Brent and Lily Ballstow snapped into place. This was just too much of a coincidence. Nick Riley was missing. Colleen Sturgis had been murdered. And with the Ballstows' connection to these two cases, their deaths could not have been murder-suicide. Which meant they were murdered too. All these tragedies connected somehow. Not accidental, but orchestrated.

"How long ago? What happened?"

"Don't quote me just yet, but from what we can tell, about forty-eight hours ago." He looked at the house, then back at her. "What was your relationship to the victim? Was she a client of yours?"

"No. We'd never actually met before. And she wasn't expecting me today. My interest in her was tangential."

"Don't think you can confuse me with your twenty-dollar words. Tell me what you're doing here."

She sighed, wishing she could just bulldoze over his questions and get her own answers. But with Noah set to go on sabbatical soon, her access to inside information was vanishing before her eyes. What kind of investigator would she be if she were stuck on the outside looking in, never able to simply ask what the authorities knew?

Maybe if she did her best to play ball and not throw so many curves, Darnell would stop hitting her pitches back in her face. For whatever reason, he needed to feel like the big dog in charge. It was in her best interest to just let him go ahead and feel that way.

For much of her FBI career, Winter had been compulsively abrasive. It was the only way to get all the boys in the club to take her seriously. It seemed that was another thing different in the private sector. Without the badge, her access to police information and resources depended as much on her reputation as it did on her ability to schmooze.

"I wanted to question Sturgis about her relationship with a known drug dealer and ex-con named Kyle Fobb."

Darnell looked at her, though his body continued to face away. "Was he her dealer?"

"I don't know for certain, since I never got to talk to her, but they'd known each other since they were in middle school together. If Sturgis was using drugs, there's a chance she might've gotten them from him."

"That house is caked in drugs." He popped his sunglasses back on. "If she was using even half of what we found, then the fact that she survived long enough to be murdered is a small miracle."

Winter folded her arms. "This is connected to the Ballstow case."

Like a statue on a pivoting pedestal, his entire body swung to face her. "I'm listening."

"Colleen Sturgis went to school with Kyle Fobb. Kyle is

the ex-husband of Jessica Huberth, who started the JCH Bloom makeup company using seed money given to her by Colleen." Winter held up a finger for each person as she named them. "One of JCH Bloom's top sellers was Lily Ballstow, who just happened to be Jessica's niece. This means at one point Kyle Fobb was Lily's uncle by marriage. And now Lily's dead and so is Colleen." She clenched her hand into a tight fist.

Behind those glasses, Winter had no idea what Darnell might be thinking. He stared at her without speaking, without moving.

"You know as well as I do there's no such thing as coincidences." Winter used her gentle voice, not the abrasive one. "No such thing as a small world."

Darnell gave another epic sigh before retrieving his phone from his pocket. "Kyle Fobb?"

"Yes. F-o-b-b." Winter nodded and whipped out her own phone to check the fact sheet Ariel had emailed her. "Kyle Benjamin Fobb. Fifty-two years old." She showed Darnell his stats and photo.

"Okay…" Darnell typed it in, checking the guy's background. "That's a decent sheet. Lots of drugs. His current address is one of those felony-friendly complexes. Police are on those like roaches on cake crumbs. But it looks like he's been keeping his nose clean since he got out two years ago."

"Clean as an ex-con drug dealer can keep it."

"Fair enough." Darnell nodded thoughtfully as he slipped his phone back into his pocket. "I'll look into him."

"Thank you." Winter had noted his home address earlier, too, when she opened her email from Ariel to get Colleen Sturgis's address. Neither one had any combination of 39584 in them.

She let her gaze drift over his shoulder toward the

commotion around the house. The nicer the neighborhood, the more people came out to watch when things went wrong. There were twice as many civilians as law enforcement and forensic techs put together. Colleen's hood was posh, so the onlookers were very polite, speaking in hushed voices and not jockeying for a view. They made light banter with the cops, trying to subtly elicit gritty details from them.

Only in a rich neighborhood.

"How did she die?" Winter asked.

"She was stabbed. I can't tell you much more than that. Forensics just arrived on the scene, and we don't have much to go on yet."

"Who called it in?"

"Her maid comes on Thursdays. When Colleen didn't answer the doorbell, the woman peeked in the window. You can literally see Sturgis's corpse swimming in a pool of blood from the front window by the door."

"Well, thank goodness for nosy maids. You got your people out combing the neighborhood?"

"Of course." Darnell shook his head. "Thank you for the information. And I'll be sure to look into Fobb. But I don't understand where your interest in this case is coming from. You don't even have a client."

"I served a guy summons papers, and the next day he was dead. You expect me to just shrug that off?"

"When you put it that way…" He cleared his throat. "I'll keep you in the loop, okay? But you need to keep me aware of what you're doing too. You can't just go around questioning people before sharing the tip with the police."

Winter lifted her shoulders. "So sue me if I want to check out a lead before I waste your time with it. I'm not keeping secrets. I thought I was doing you a favor."

"Me, a favor?" He scoffed, but there was a tiny curl in his lip, not unlike a smile.

"What updates have there been on Nick Riley's disappearance?"

"Since we found his car? Nothing. Oh, except that was his blood in it. We were able to get into his apartment through his mom to grab DNA to compare."

The fact that he knew exactly who and what she was talking about told Winter he'd been racking his brain to connect everything too. That up until Colleen Sturgis's death, he probably thought Brent Ballstow killed Nick Riley before offing his wife and himself out of guilt.

Colleen Sturgis. It didn't make any sense.

One of the officers called Davenport over. As he turned and walked away, Winter decided she'd be better off cutting out early than hanging back and massaging details out of any of the other cops.

It had been a long while since one of her interactions with Detective Davenport had ended on a high note, and she didn't want to ruin it by overstaying her welcome.

26

My damn phone was dead, and I didn't have a charger. I always overlooked little details like that. My ex-wife used to go off on me over my spaced-out brain. Used to question if I even had a brain half the time. I hated it when she talked to me like that.

I already knew I was stupid. My mom had engrained that into me. She'd come home really late, and I'd be up waiting for her, watching TV. I'd run to greet her, and she'd smack me in the face for getting ketchup on her nice dress.

When I got home from driving past Colleen's house for the tenth time since I'd killed her, the first thing I did was charge my phone. When it popped on, I saw the boss had texted me multiple times.

Where are you?
Dammit!!!! I told you to text me when the cops found Colleen!!!!
Why aren't you answering?
How do you expect me to stay on top of this if I don't have all the facts all the time?!
I swear to god...

My heart got tight reading them. I was in big trouble. I

took a deep breath to pull my shit together. When that didn't work, I loaded up the pipe on the table and took a big rip.

In seconds, my anxiety began to transform, and I found the courage to text the boss.

The maid showed up earlier today, and now there's cops all over the place. It just happened.

My numb fingers shook on the phone as I watched the three little dots bounce around.

Yes, I know!

Her next message came in on the heels of her last one.

Where the hell have you been?!

Nowhere.

I could hear the boys working downstairs in the basement, cooking up the next batch for the boss and pushers to sell.

Is that all you have to say for yourself? Wtf...

I'm sorry.

She messaged back with an angry little swearing emoji.

Just do as you're told when you're told and everything will be fine.

I bit my lip. The pot was making me brave as my thumbs continued typing.

I don't understand why we had to off our backer if she was such an important part of the business. I mean, she financed us and helped us find all our top-grossing clients. You said so yourself. I know she screwed up, but we took care of that. We didn't have to kill her too.

You don't have to understand! Are you saying you doubt the plan?

I don't even know the plan! If that plan is to leave town, let's go!

After I sent my message, I waited for the three dots to start their dance. They didn't. A wave of anxiety hit me like a wall of bricks. Then an incoming call shook me, and I flinched so hard that I dropped the phone.

When I picked it up, the screen had a hairline crack. But

it was still ringing—the boss. She was calling. I knew she was about to rip me a new one. It was the only reason she ever called.

I swiped to answer and swallowed the swelling balloon in my throat. "Hello?"

"I already explained this to you, but given your tiny brain can't seem to retain information longer than a couple of minutes, I'm going to explain it again."

She was seething, but I was happy to hear her voice anyway.

"The fewer people who know the plan, the better. I know why Colleen had to die, and I know exactly what happens next and why. Your job is to trust me and do what you're told, understand?"

"Yes. I know my job. Me and my boys make or buy the drugs in bulk, and you distribute them. I know you've got everything set up nicely, but Colleen brought us so many new customers."

"You always had a thing for her."

"I never did! I've told you." I really was going to throw up now. "I literally stabbed her to death, and you're still trying to act like I'm into her. None of this was what I wanted. All I want is my life back. My love. My marriage."

"Well, that's never going to happen so long as you keep making stupid mistakes!"

My heart lurched in my chest like somebody was twisting a fork into it. "I did exactly what you told me to do! What mistakes are you talking about?"

"Not telling me about the cops at Colleen's and the Ballstows', you idiot!" Her voice dripped venom. "I just saw a report that there's been a break in the case."

"A break?" My numb lips had trouble forming the words because my heart was still being forked to death. "I don't understand."

"You never do." She laughed. "An unnamed outside source has provided investigators with new information. Which means they're still investigating the Ballstows. Which means they don't think Brent did it."

"Are you sure?"

"Of course I'm sure! I don't know why the hell I thought I could trust you with this. Of course you screwed it up, just like you do everything."

"Please don't say that…" My ribs were beginning to ache, my heart pounding them to powder. "I did my best."

"You held the gun in Brent's hand?"

"Yes."

"And you killed the wife first?"

"Of course."

"And you made sure the angle was natural?"

"Yes! I did everything you said."

"You didn't do something so stupid even I couldn't predict it? Like retrieve the bullets from the scene or try to clean up the blood…"

"No! I promise, I swear. There's nothing to link their deaths back to us. It's impossible."

"Well, they found something. Which means you screwed up. Not to mention, you couldn't even handle keeping Nick alive!"

I didn't want to tell her that I still had him locked down in my well. That I sort of lied, and he was still alive. I heard him again last night. And I definitely didn't want to tell her that I was too afraid to fish him out. "You said you were happy he was dead."

"That's not the point! The point is you're useless."

The line went dead. She'd hung up, just like I knew she would.

I threw the phone across the room so hard that, when it hit a side table lamp, they both crashed to the floor. But I didn't give a damn. A man could only endure so much, and I'd had enough.

Still, as I took another rip from the bong, I replayed the events of the murder-suicide in my mind over and over. Cops always had the upper hand because all a killer had to do was make one tiny mistake in the moment, while the cops could spend a whole lifetime trying to find it.

What had I done wrong? The TV? I'd worn my gloves and bandanna so as to not leave any DNA or fingerprints at the scene. I locked up afterward. But what if I messed up? What if I'd left some of my hair on the couch when I sat down next to Brent? What if they'd somehow noticed that he'd been choked out before the shots were fired?

My slow brain was firing as fast as it ever had, but beyond all the noise, a single question sounded over all the others.

Did she mean what she'd said? Had I made so many stupid mistakes that I'd never get the love of my life back like she'd promised?

I couldn't let that happen. Whatever mistakes I'd made in the past, I was going to fix them. And if I couldn't, then all I needed was one more bullet.

27

Darnell had said he'd look into Kyle Fobb, and Winter trusted him to keep his word. That didn't mean she was ready to let go of the reins just yet. He also said to loop him in, and she had her own little researcher on the case.

After she pulled away from the murder scene that marred Colleen Sturgis's fancy neighborhood, she made her way to Kyle Fobb's downtown apartment.

The place might as well have had a twenty-foot chain-link fence with barbed wire circling the top. It was basic and open like a motel, and she'd seen three cop cars circle the block in the fifteen minutes she'd sat curbside. There was nothing going on there, but she was an investigator with questions.

Winter got out and knocked on his second floor door. No one appeared to be home. But the curtains to the main living area, if it deserved such a grandiose name, weren't pulled shut, so she peeked in. It was sparsely furnished, with not so much as a glass on a surface or a piece of mail anywhere.

Winter went back to her Pilot and called Ariel over the speaker.

When she answered, she sounded flustered and out of breath. "Black Investigations, please hold."

"Ariel—"

But she wasn't quick enough. The line crackled and clicked, and their hold music came on.

Winter sighed and waited, drumming her fingers on the steering wheel to the oldie but goody. She did often find herself caught between the moon and, well, not so much New York City, but Austin these days. Definitely. It was a nice metaphor for how cases generally felt before most of the evidence was tracked down, putting the puzzle together.

Five minutes later, the line clicked and started to ring again, just like Winter had programmed it to do.

"Black Investigations. Thank you for holding."

"Ariel? Is everything okay?"

"Oh, hey, Winter." There was an odd twitter in her voice. A breathlessness like she'd just been caught out on a run. "Everything's fine. Just the phone's been ringing off the hook, and…do you have any idea when Kline will be back from his vacation?"

"I'm not sure…" She hadn't told Ariel where Kline had gone or what had happened to him since he'd been there. "Why do you ask? I don't think he'd be much help answering phones."

"That freaking toilet." Winter could all but see Ariel speaking through clenched teeth. "The leak is getting worse. When I flushed it earlier, water started to spread out from the base. I got the floor in there covered with a roll of paper towels."

"Call a plumber. We can't wait for Kline."

For all I know, he might end up indicted for murder and never come back to Austin.

Winter grimaced. She didn't want to believe it. But just like every other time she'd thought about her biological father's predicament in the last few days, she could not avoid conjuring negative outcomes.

"I need your help. Can you do a lookup on Kyle Fobb and—"

"I sent you his address."

"Breathe, Ariel. Do a lookup for former addresses and other family ties. And where does the guy work?"

"Yeah, okay. Just a second."

Before Winter could ask her not to, Ariel put her back on hold. The song picked up right where she'd left it, and Winter was drumming her fingers again.

Well, at least the hold music's effective, keeping us antsy 'on holders' distracted and relaxed.

As she waited, unable to help herself humming along to the early eighties ballad and cursing herself all the while, Winter couldn't help but wonder about the state Ariel was in. The young woman had a lot of talent for investigation. A quick mind that asked the right questions and churned over details other people would miss.

But if she got this flustered over a busy phone and leaky toilet, what chance did she have of making it as a private investigator? It wasn't an overstatement to say the job could be a bit stressful from time to time.

The line clicked and Ariel came back on. "Hi. So Kyle Fobb apparently collects disability for a back injury he incurred prior to prison. And he has two grown sons and two ex-wives. He's lived in that same felony-friendly apartment since getting out."

"Where do his sons live?"

"Troy Fobb is at…huh. He doesn't seem to have an address. Let's see about Michael Fobb."

Winter sang along to the chorus of the old pop tune while she waited.

"Double huh."

"What?"

"He doesn't have an address either."

"Okay, how about the name of Kyle's first wife? The kids are likely hers. Maybe they live there."

"They're like twentysomething but okay. Her name is Faye Anne Fobb. And nothing. She doesn't live anywhere either."

"Got a maiden name?"

"Faye Anne Diddam. One past address in Austin. This was two decades ago. Not sure what good this'll do, but it's 39584 Maple Trail."

The numbers hit Winter like a hammer in her guts. "Say again."

"The address is 39584 Maple Trail…"

Winter dug in her purse for the catalog she'd found at Lily's house and narrowed her eyes at the numbers scribbled on the back. Kyle's address. That was what the red glow had been trying to lead her to, not Jessica Huberth at JCH Bloom.

"When will you be back at the office?" Ariel asked.

"As soon as I can." Winter chewed on her lip. Deep down, she knew that answers about what happened to Brent and Lily Ballstow would be waiting for her at Kyle Fobb's first wife's house, where, she guessed, Kyle and his sons were.

"You think the grown-ass kids never moved out of their childhood home?"

That was exactly what she was thinking. "Thank you, Ariel, for the information and the commentary."

"Be careful out there." Ariel's voice was suddenly gentle. "And don't get yourself killed. I need this job."

Winter snorted at the joke. It was in poor taste, but she preferred her jokes that way. Besides, what more could she expect from an overworked administrative assistant having to run the ship with a leaky toilet?

"Love you, too, Ariel. I'll talk to you soon."

She hit a button on the steering wheel and hung up.

This was the part where she was supposed to call for backup. But who would that be exactly? Noah was out of town fighting his own good fight. Ariel was about to lose her crap over a freaking leaky toilet. And Darnell, well…

She could call him. She should call him. Dammit, she *would* call him. There was a chance he'd be irritated and tell her not to go. When she didn't follow his orders—imagine him feeling entitled to give her orders!—he might get irritated and follow after or send a patrol to take over. Either way, Kyle Fobb would get the scrutiny he deserved.

Three people had been murdered. Getting justice for them was all that really mattered, whatever way they eventually came around to it. Whether it was her or APD that solved the case in the end was secondary.

Before she could talk herself out of it, she called Darnell. The call connected and rang, her heart rising and falling with the tone, until at last a voice came on the line.

"Hello, you have reached Detective Darnell Davenport with the Austin Police Department. If this is an emergency, please hang up and dial 911. Otherwise, leave your name and number, and I will get back to you."

After the beep, she left a message. "Darnell, I'm headed over to 39584 Maple Trail. It's where I believe Kyle Fobb and his sons are residing. I want to talk to Kyle." She quickly double-checked his address and read it out loud again. "I really think he's our guy. Can you come meet up with me? Otherwise, I'll call you within the hour to tell you what I found out."

Winter hung up and gripped the steering wheel so hard her knuckles turned white. She still had no real clue just what the hell was going on or why.

Kyle Fobb had a strong connection to Colleen Sturgis and was connected to Lily Ballstow through her aunt, Jessica

Huberth of JCH Bloom. But she couldn't figure out what Kyle's motivation would be for killing either woman or, by extension, Lily's husband Brent. But assuming Kyle Fobb was the killer—and based on the red glow and his sketchy past, that was exactly where she was leaning—he needed motivation to hurt these people.

Sturgis, in particular, seemed strange. Drug dealers didn't usually kill their most profitable customers.

And what about Nick Riley? His disappearance could be a fluke, or a wrench in the overall plan. Still, a guy who was suing Brent Ballstow went missing days before Brent, Lily, and Colleen were killed. It had to be part of the equation.

Winter's brain spiraled, trying to make the puzzle pieces fit. Kyle, Jessica, Colleen, and Lily were all connected through JCH Bloom. Brent was married to Lily, so he could have easily become collateral damage. Sure, Nick Riley was suing Brent Ballstow…but she couldn't connect him directly to JCH Bloom at all.

To put it another way, what did an appliance company, a makeup company, and a drug dealer have in common?

She held up her hand and ticked down a finger for each item she knew for sure. The well-established appliance company was in need of money.

The young MLM makeup company seemed to be swimming in it.

And the drug dealer seemed to be the man killing everyone.

Winter balled her hand into a fist. Why?

And Colleen Sturgis—an uber-wealthy addict who gave Jessica Huberth the money to start the makeup enterprise—was also dead.

She punched the steering wheel lightly. Again, why?

If Kyle was dealing drugs again, it didn't make sense to Winter that he would kill a big client with a bad habit and an endless supply of money, or that he would also kill JCH Bloom's number two earner, Lily Ballstow. What did the women have in common besides their connection to JCH Bloom? Lily did not look like an addict at all, and neither did Brent.

Winter took a deep breath and opened her fist. When murderers killed people they knew, the motive was normally about relationships or money. Lily seemed to be loyal to Brent. They both seemed devoted. She guessed there could've been an affair going on between Colleen and Kyle. But there'd have to be a third party involved to kill over love —the notorious love triangle.

Winter had a feeling she was about to find out the answers to all her questions. Kyle Fobb didn't seem to be living in his apartment. He didn't have a place of work. His sons had no known residences, and that left one place for her to look—at the address that was flagged specially for her. She started her SUV.

Whether Kyle Fobb actually turned out to be the killer or not, he was clearly the key to this whole situation. And Winter was on her way to pry open the lock.

28

GPS led Winter outside of Austin's city limits. There were horses and cattle being raised in large, fenced-in pastures. She passed fields of hay, sorghum, corn, and pecans. Eventually, she came to a remote area where the houses were settled in a beautiful expanse of virgin forest, each with surrounding property of at least a couple of acres.

Winter turned off the two-lane highway onto the twisted gravel road called Maple Trail. Her wireless connection went out, and she trundled along at a snail's pace, checking the numbers printed on the mailboxes lining the road in front of each little farmhouse and cabin she passed. When she saw the address she was looking for—39584—she slowed, rolling down the road a few dozen yards before drifting to a stop across the street.

So as to not alarm the residents, she parked so they wouldn't be able to see her Honda from their porch. Then she killed the engine.

With forest-green shingles on the roof and a wraparound porch, complete with intricate latticing and a large bay window, the house looked like it had once been adorable. But the whitewash was chipped, the lattice was broken in many places, and winding vines crept over a full side of the house, anchoring it to the land.

The lawn was overgrown but verdant with the recent rain. Tiny white flowers bloomed alongside wild bluebonnets. The sun had just come out from playing hide-and-seek, and raindrops twinkled on the leaves.

A broken window on the second floor gave her pause, and she wondered if the house was abandoned. It didn't seem like anybody had cared about it in a very long time.

After waiting for a trailer carting horses to pass by, Winter crossed the road and picked her way along the overgrown path toward the front door of 39584 Maple Trail. She noted abandoned vehicles reposed in the tall grass, rusting and slowly surrendering to nature.

A chill paused her tread, and she focused on the weight of the .38 strapped in the ankle holster inside her left leg. A newly acquired backup piece, that she was grateful—for the second time that week—to have purchased.

When she mounted the stairs to the porch, the wood creaked in pain. As she did, things were starting to fall in place in Winter's mind.

Brent Ballstow was in need of money that JCH Bloom—a company his wife worked for—had. And Lily had this address on the back of a JCH Bloom catalog. So it stood to reason Lily Ballstow was going to blackmail her ex-Uncle Kyle somehow for money. In doing so, she got herself and Brent killed. But how did Colleen fit in? Or Nick?

Winter inched her finger forward to ring the bell before noticing the wires that ran to it had been cut.

It was now or never…

Winter balled a fist and knocked on the door.

❋

Noah and Eve took a late lunch in a little hole-in-the-wall taqueria with three-dollar margaritas and two-dollar street tacos. Eve sipped on a Mexican brew while Noah stared out at the gray streets.

The rain had stopped at around the same time the raid did, but the sun had yet to peek out. An old woman walked down the road with her unleashed chihuahua, the edge of her stomach hanging out from the bottom of her shirt and swaying with her steps.

He and Eve both knew this was going to be their last assignment together for at least a year and maybe ever, depending on what Noah ended up doing. The tension of that truth hung in the air like black fog, stifling attempts at conversation.

"Did you know I never had a choice about joining the FBI?" Eve asked after a long silence.

Noah furrowed his brow. "What do you mean?"

"My great-great-grandfather was one of the first thirty-four agents working under Charles Bonaparte and President Teddy Roosevelt before the official Bureau of Investigation was even named. My great-grandfather was an agent, too, and in 1972, when women were allowed to join up, my grandmother was one of the first. My mother still works for the Bureau as a consultant, and my father was CIA. My career path was set out for me long before I was even born."

Noah opened his eyes wide at this. "Wow. That's one hell of a genealogy. Must've been an interesting way to grow up."

Eve shrugged. Her long blond hair was scattered in limp, wet strings around her shoulders, and her eyes looked pale gray in the miserable light. "It's not that different from growing up with parents who are grifters or celebrities. When you're a kid, you assume whatever your family is like is normal, no matter how weird they might actually be. And by the time you grow up and realize the truth, it *is* normal to you. You were raised the way you were raised."

Noah nodded. "Yeah, that makes sense."

"My mother didn't want me to join the Bureau. She tried to convince me to do anything else." Eve looked out the window. "In high school, I was really into wrestling. She thought I ought to become a coach."

"That's unusual." Noah took a big bite of his pork belly taco.

"I thought it was, too, at the time. I never really understood. But when I went into the Bureau, she supported me. She still supports me. But now, I wonder about my own little goblins." Eve took a sip of her beer. "Before they were born, I assumed they'd just follow me and the rest of the family into the Bureau. But the second I held my first baby in my arms and saw for myself how helpless and precious she was, I changed my mind."

"Why?"

Eve set down her beer. "You don't have any kids, but I know you can understand what it's like to love someone and not want them to get hurt. The path we walk in life is dangerous, strewn with bullets and uncertainty. Every day, we see and hear about things that would give anybody nightmares." She shook her head and looked down into her bottle. "I don't want my kids to follow in my footsteps."

Her words landed heavily on Noah's shoulders. All he could think about was Winter on her own out there doing who knew what.

Eve popped a pickled jalapeño into her mouth. "Do you think you and Winter will ever have kids?"

"I..." Noah had no idea how to answer that. Part of him had always wanted a family, and the thought of Winter as a mother made him feel all warm and squishy inside. But then he remembered Justin and his cadre of loyal, psychotic fans.

And all the evil men and women over the years who'd tried to hurt him and Winter.

He thought of the van with all those little boys and girls with ghosts hiding behind their eyes.

How could he justify bringing kids into this world? He already felt helpless against fate and circumstance, far more often than he would ever admit out loud. Simply worrying about his wife's safety was driving him to distraction. If there was a tiny human in the mix, he might never be able to keep his head in the game. He'd be paralyzed by fear and anxiety.

Noah's dad had walked out on him when he was a kid, leaving him to figure out how to be a man all on his own. He'd always promised himself that if he ever did have kids, they'd never know what that felt like. They'd never have to feel so painfully lonely, wondering what was wrong with them that even their own father couldn't stick around to love them. He intended to be the kind of dad that was so consummately there for his kids that they took him for granted.

With his job the way it was—the way it had been for so long—he hadn't been in a position where he could entertain the idea of starting a family.

"We've never really talked about it," Noah said at last.

"Might be a good time to broach the subject while you're on sabbatical." Eve smiled weakly. "I hope you're able to make the most of this while you're gone. Take some time to do a little soul searching. Go on vacation. You have a unique opportunity in front of you."

He nodded, a beam of hope breaking into his foreboding inner landscape like dawn over the mountains. "You're right."

"I guess you're probably planning on helping Winter out, yeah? Try on the private investigator hat."

"Definitely."

"Good luck with that. I'm pretty sure my husband and I would kill each other if we spent that much time together."

Noah often forgot about Eve's husband and kids. "You don't talk about him much."

"It's not really appropriate to be going on and on about your spouse when you're supposed to be working." Eve smiled, razzing him. "Besides, my husband's a very private person. He works from home, takes care of the kids, never really gets himself in any trouble. Best of all, he has absolutely nothing to do with law enforcement."

Noah sighed wistfully. "I envy you that."

"Give me a break." Eve snorted. "You love your crazy vigilante wife."

"Of course I do. That doesn't mean I don't wish Winter would stop getting herself in trouble."

"Well, from now on, you'll be there to keep an eye on her. At least for the next year."

Though he nodded, he privately wondered if it would be enough. He'd been doing his best to keep an eye on her when Justin swooped in and kidnapped her from under his nose. Even if he was at her side and spent every ounce of his energy keeping her safe, she could still slip through his fingers.

"To new beginnings." Eve lifted her beer and smiled.

Noah picked up his water glass and tapped it against the bottle. "And to our spouses. What would we do without them?"

"A lot more cooking for one." Eve said with a laugh.

"My own laundry," Noah chimed in.

"Nice, you win."

He did win. When it came to Winter, he'd won the lottery.

29

Winter knocked again on the heavy wooden door. Nothing.

She surveyed the porch. Like the rest of the house, it badly needed to be sanded down and repainted. A pile of dust and junk in the far corner drew her attention, where hundreds of cigarette butts had collected on top of what looked like old hypodermic needles. A catalog poked out of the top of an open garbage bag, and Winter caught sight of a flourish of golden letters scrawled across the top.

JCH Bloom.

A chill ran down her spine. Kyle Fobb was connected to JCH Bloom, and not just as the ex-husband of the CEO.

Kyle was back to using drugs now that he was out of prison, though on paper he sure looked clean. How was he pulling that off? By keeping an apartment in good standing in the city. By using his sons' childhood home to cook meth. A home that belonged to his untraceable first wife, Faye.

And by pushing his drug supply through the makeup company.

Winter's mind was spinning now, like it always did when the fragmented pieces of an investigation started gravitating toward one another. It made the most sense. Though JCH Bloom was only a few years old, they'd been abundantly successful from the onset. No growing pains.

Lily Ballstow might've caught on to Aunt Jessica's real MLM scheme, that the makeup company was a beard for a drug enterprise. Maybe Lily had gone to Kyle's and smelled what Winter was smelling and figured it all out, then tried to extort money for Brent and all his legal fees by threatening to turn her ex-uncle back over to the authorities. If she did do that, the whole MLM would go under without their supplier.

Another possible angle was that Lily knew JCH Bloom was peddling narcotics because she was a pusher. She just didn't know who the supplier was. If that were true, those sunshine-and-smiles salespeople Amy Powell and Sybil Huberth could also be drug-delivery women.

There was a lot to unpack.

Winter glanced behind her toward where she knew her car was parked. She should go.

Just as that thought took hold, she heard commotion inside—a sound like footsteps.

The door flew open, and a man stood before her. He was in his mid-twenties, skinny as a rail and drowning in a black t-shirt over a pair of boxers that looked just as loose. His skin was sickly pale, his cheeks sunken and gaunt. He was barefooted, and his toenails were super thick and cloudy yellow, looking like they hadn't been clipped in months. A lit cigarette hung from the corner of his crusty lips.

It wasn't Kyle Fobb as she had hoped, but the man sure resembled him. Had to be Troy or Michael.

The chemical smell rushed at Winter through the door, assaulting her senses. She forced herself not to wrinkle her nose. "Hi." She smiled pleasantly. "I'm sorry to bother you.

My GPS is on the fritz, and I'm lost. Could you give me directions back to the highway?"

He eyed her up and down, then took a deep pull on his cigarette and blew the foul-smelling smoke in her face. "Hang on."

He turned and disappeared inside the house. Winter was granted a single brief image of the interior before he closed the door all but an inch. A rickety fan blowing near an open window. A coffee table covered in clutter with the shaft of a tall blue bong sticking up above the mess.

The door swung open again, and Winter wheeled back to see the barrel of a shotgun pointed in her face.

"Get in the house." The skinny man snapped the words like firecrackers.

Winter put her hands up. "I'm sorry. I'll go. I just needed directions."

"Horseshit." He kicked the door behind him wide open with the flat of a bare foot. "Get your ass in the house now."

She looked at the gun, then inside the dark, foul-smelling house. She did not want to go in there. Her own gun was still strapped in a holster on her ankle. But she couldn't get to it with her palms in the air.

Winter blinked, conjuring tears. "Please. Just let me go back to my car. You'll never see me again. I swear."

"Troy!" a man's voice called from inside the house. "Where the hell are you? You were supposed to bring the damn gasoline."

"Mikey!" the man with the gun shouted back. "C'mere!"

A moment later, the second man appeared in the front room. Though Mikey was taller than Troy and much heavier, both men had inherited Kyle's Greek nose and his dark, narrow-set eyes.

Mikey was dressed in denim coveralls, like a painter might wear, with goggles on his head and a gas mask hanging around his neck. A long scar cut down one of his cheeks and split the corner of his lips. And on his other cheek, near his left eye, three black dots were tattooed.

When Mikey saw Winter, his dark eyes narrowed into cruel slits. "Who's this bitch?"

"Says she needs directions." Troy shrugged, keeping the shotgun trained on her head. At this range, the force of the blast would pop her skull like two fingernails to a ripe zit.

"I'll give her directions to my nut sack." Mikey grabbed his crotch just in case she was confused about the location of his balls.

This was bad. This was really bad and getting worse by the second. One thing Winter knew for sure—if she went inside that house, she'd never come back out.

The sound of an engine coming down the road brought a surge of hope. They couldn't just stand there on the porch with a gun trained on her face for everybody to see. She glanced back, moving her eyes but not her head, and saw gravel and dust flying around a rusted-out white pickup truck.

The truck pulled up to the drive, and a man got out, slapping the door closed behind him. "What the hell are you doing, asshole?"

Troy shrugged. "She just turned up out of nowhere."

"Can we keep her?" Mikey smiled to reveal rotten yellow-and-brown teeth.

Winter knew a case of meth mouth when she saw one.

The gas mask, the chemical smell, and the prison tattoo were all strong clues, but the teeth were a dead giveaway. Meth. Unfortunately, she'd interrupted their operation mid-cook, it appeared.

The man from the truck jogged up the stairs and into her line of view. Dressed in a flimsy flannel shirt that was open over a graying undershirt and khaki cargo pants, he looked to be in his mid-fifties. He was wiry, nothing but muscle and bones, and taller than the other two. He wore a faded red bandanna tied over his hair so she couldn't see what color it was—but there were those beady black eyes, same as his boys. Kyle Fobb looked taller in person than he did in his online photo.

A tattoo of a playing card—the queen of hearts—adorned one of his forearms. One of the queen's heads looked standard, a flower delicately grasped in her white hand. The upside-down queen's face was a skeleton with a bloodied knife in her grip, and the heart near her face was broken.

Winter sniffled, trying to look small and harmless and frightened like she assumed any normal woman would if they were caught in her situation. "Please." Her voice cracked. "I just want to get back to the highway."

"Get that outta her face." Kyle stepped up beside Troy and set his fingertips on the barrel of the gun, encouraging him to lower it. "Don't mind these two morons. Troy here would point a gun at a kitten if it showed up unexpected."

Winter nodded quickly, her breath shaking as she swatted at her fake tears. But she was relieved to have the gun off her —though aware it could be raised again just as easily.

"Don't cry, honey. That's all right." The older man set his hand on her shoulder, and there was almost something gentle about it. Kyle Fobb—Lily Ballstow's ex-uncle and Jessica Huberth's ex-husband—surprised her with that move.

It seemed absurd at first, but if she squinted, she could almost see the two of them together. Kyle was ruggedly handsome in his weird, wiry way, and Winter could imagine Jessica slumming it with this guy, back before she was a cosmetics queen.

Winter had come here to question him. That now seemed like the worst idea she'd ever had.

"Can I go?"

Kyle looked at her, his mouth slightly open, and he chewed on the tip of his tongue with his back teeth. He tilted his head curiously to one side.

She did not like the way he was looking at her.

"I know you."

Winter swallowed hard. She could make a run for it, but the loaded shotgun was still at the ready in Troy's hand. She could never get back to her vehicle before he took her down.

"I've never seen you before."

Kyle shook his head. Then the light of recognition dawned in his eyes. "You're that chick I saw talking to Holly at Lily's house."

30

Winter's eyes widened. How could this man have seen her at Lily Ballstow's? She'd only been there twice, and both times very briefly. Once, when she served Brent the papers, and again, when she talked to Lily's sister and found the glowing catalog. No one else had been around either time.

Winter was pathologically aware of her surroundings. When she'd served Brent, there'd been a gardener a few houses down doing edging in a backyard. No joggers, no dog-walkers, no lookie-loos. And she definitely would've noticed a guy who looked like Kyle Fobb hanging around in a posh neighborhood like the one where the Ballstows lived.

"Who are you really?" Kyle snatched a pistol from his waistband, cocked it, and pointed it at her forehead. "What are you doing here?"

Reading the other man's cues, Troy raised the shotgun and pointed it back in her face.

Winter gritted her teeth as the full reality of her situation constricted around her. She was standing face-to-face with the man who'd shot Brent and Lily Ballstow. The man who'd stabbed Colleen Sturgis to death.

He must've been watching the house when she'd stopped by and met Holly—keeping his eye on the investigation.

Kyle Fobb had all but confessed to being Brent and Lily Ballstow's killer. Why he killed Colleen Sturgis was still unclear. But maybe he'd tell her that, too, in the next thirty seconds. A woman could dream.

Winter was trapped. If she was going to die here, she at least wanted to understand why.

"I asked you a question!" Kyle barked.

Winter's gaze darted around the porch and the corners of the house. The yard was coated in weeds with spiny tips, many rising taller than waist height. They could give her some cover, but her Honda was too far away. To get to it, she'd have to cross this quarter-acre front lawn and the road, all while going through the arduous process of retrieving her keys and starting up the engine while two men shot at her.

The SUV was a lost cause. The house was surrounded by woods. If she could somehow get around the side of the house without getting shot, she would be able to get her gun out. Then she might have a chance.

That was a big *if*. A gun fired by an idiot could kill a person just as easily as a gun fired by an expert. That was one of the many inherent problems with guns, which made them so much more dangerous than any other weapon in history.

One bullet could kill. Winter didn't want to risk making a run for it if she didn't absolutely have to.

"Don't shoot me." She kept her words measured and slow.

Troy spat onto the porch, his crusty lips curling. "Why the hell not?"

As she contemplated her situation, a strange wave of calm swept over her. This unlooked-for serenity often arose in these kinds of tense situations, yet another unintended consequence of all she'd been through in her life.

She could be paralyzed with indecision in the grocery

store, her heart thrumming like a kick drum. But throw her into a hellscape with three drug addicts, two with guns, and she'd experience a heightened sense of herself. Time would stand still, as was happening now. She became intensely aware of her body, from the way her ankles were bent to the tension in her fingers.

First, she would try to talk her way out. Every syllable would buy her more time as she prepared to fight or flee.

"My husband knows I'm here. He'll come looking for me. He'll find the blood on your front porch…"

Why hadn't she called Noah to let him know where she would be? Even if he couldn't come meet her.

Winter couldn't remember the last time she'd felt more alone than she did right now. Back in Richmond, she'd had a huge team of people backing her up at every moment. How had she let herself become so isolated?

At least she'd called Darnell. He'd come for her. She knew he would.

On the other hand, she'd said she'd call within the hour, and only thirty minutes had passed.

Kyle Fobb's features twisted with rage. "Are you threatening me, missy?"

"I'm just telling you what will happen." Winter straightened her neck.

"We'll just kill you in the backyard then."

"It doesn't have to go down this way. Please. Just give me a chance to explain."

Kyle lifted his brows. "I'm listening."

Funny how often she said *I can explain* before having any idea what she was going to say. "Can you put the guns down first?"

He snorted and readjusted his aim on her. She'd known it was unlikely.

A dozen different possible excuses flipped through her

head like a spinning wheel. She considered telling him that Jessica had sent her but didn't know how he might react to the mention of his ex-wife's name. Maybe bringing up a friend would be more innocuous.

"Colleen sent me."

Kyle Fobb's face paled and then reddened in the space of a second. "Colleen sent you?"

The ammonia and bleach smell stabbed at Winter's nostrils. "She told me you could sell me some tweak."

"Did she?"

By the look on his face, Winter knew right away that was the wrong thing to say too. Again, her gaze darted to the corner of the house, then back to the shotgun.

"You don't look like no tweaker to me." Kyle stepped closer and pressed the cold barrel of his pistol against Winter's temple. "You look like you live in the suburbs."

She did, technically. But anybody familiar with statistics on methamphetamine usage could tell you those two things were not mutually exclusive. "If by suburbs you mean Colleen's neighborhood, I wish. The doctors took away my Adderall."

"I think you're full of shit."

"I swear. I don't want any trouble. Colleen told me you could help me out."

"Mikey, search her."

The burly guy stepped forward with a hungry expression.

Winter kept her hands raised as he slid his hands over her hips and torso, brushing her breasts. Her insides burned with a passionate need to break both his arms, but the two guns pointed at her face prevented her.

He found her wallet in her back pocket and pulled out her ID, which sat right next to her government-indorsed P.I. credentials. Which, in a way, was perfect, as it distracted him from sliding his hands down each of her legs and finding her pistol.

Mikey handed everything over to Kyle, who passed his gun to him. He then trained on her while Daddy sifted through her wallet.

Kyle gritted his teeth. "She's a cop."

"I'm not a cop. I'm a P.I. I mostly investigate insurance fraud and do paperwork." Facts. "I'm not working with the cops."

Kyle threw her wallet down on the ground and stomped closer, so his face was practically touching hers. The intense smell of mint and tobacco on his breath was nauseating. "Then who are you working for?"

"No one! I don't have any interest in whatever's going on here. Colleen hired me for an identity theft problem she had a while back, and we kind of became friends. When I asked her if she knew where I could get some tweak, she told me her friend Kyle could help me out. You're Kyle, right?"

He snarled in such a way as to confirm everything she already knew. "If Colleen sent you here, she wasn't your friend." He turned to the two younger men. "Pick up that damn wallet, boy, and bring it to me, then take her out back and finish her."

Winter's eyes widened. So much for trying to talk her way out.

As Mikey moved past her off the porch to grab her wallet from the weeds, Winter snatched Kyle by the arms of his flannel. Using the oldest judo move in the book, she wrapped her ankle over his Achilles tendon and tripped him. As Kyle lurched backward, she used the leverage of his own body weight to throw him hard into Troy. When the two men collided, the shotgun fired, tearing a splintered hole in the roof of the porch.

Winter turned to run just as Mikey barreled back up the

porch steps, swooped down, and caught a fistful of her hair in his meaty fingers. She yelped in pain as he tried dragging her, but she managed to throw an elbow back into his face. Blood sprayed like aerosol. He fell back off the steps, grabbing at his nose as he fired the gun blindly into the sky.

While she was grappling with Mikey, Troy and Kyle righted themselves, and Kyle lunged at her. His chest slammed into her back, and she stumbled. She bent at the knees to keep her balance as he lunged at a foot and yanked her down so forcefully that the air was knocked from her lungs.

"Dad, move!" Troy wailed.

She kicked behind her, hitting Kyle's head somewhere, and he released her.

"Grab her, dammit!" he screamed.

With blood oozing down his face, Mikey hoisted himself back up from the weeds and threw his weight at her. Winter rolled to one side—down and off the porch steps—as the burly guy tried to slam on top of her. He knocked his forehead hard on the last step.

Kyle was over the porch railing and in her path.

"Dad, you're blocking my fucking shot again!" Troy screamed.

Winter slammed the flat of her palm up into Kyle's nose with all her strength. The move was incapacitating if done right, but Kyle moved his head at the last moment so it didn't quite knock him out. Still, his nose cracked, and blood spewed. Tears rolled down his cheeks as he reeled in pain.

Winter raced away through the waist-high weeds.

The shotgun blasted, deafening her. Pain bit into her left arm and shoulder like a thousand stinging wasps. She stumbled but didn't stop running until she was around the side of the house.

Winter ripped her gun out of her ankle holster and

steadied it in her hands, searching for comfort in its weight. Then she glanced at her arm and shoulder.

A huge spray of black spots and blood covered the area. Bird shot.

The pain was in the back of her neck, too, but somehow her wounds weren't distracting. If anything, Winter felt more focused. She rested her good shoulder against the rickety siding, her eyes darting back and forth as she tried to plan her next move.

31

There was no time for triage. The Fobb men were already coming, ready to execute Winter for the crime of knocking on their door.

Having angled around the corner of the house, Winter took two shots to slow them down.

One bullet went wild. The other hit Mikey in the knee. Clutching his wound, he fell to his knees before rolling onto his back, groaning in pain. Kyle must've found the pistol, because he stalked after her, gun firing, undaunted by the prospect of being shot himself.

A bullet bit into the side of the house less than an inch from her head. Winter pulled back, pressing a hand to her chest.

This guy had shot Lily Ballstow right between the eyes while sitting on the couch. Winter was lucky Kyle hadn't been holding the gun when she'd made a break for it.

Forcing her legs into action, Winter ran around the back of the house and scanned for a hiding spot.

A red glow caught her eye, momentarily arresting her

attention. Her breath caught in her chest. At the far end of the yard near where the turf met the tree line, the large glow was shining from the ground. She couldn't see what it was beyond the overgrown weeds, and there was no time to check it out.

The woods were too far to run to get away from a sharpshooter like Kyle Fobb, so Winter dived under the rickety deck. Spider webs caught on her hair and face as she crawled over prickly weeds and gravel. On her hands and knees, she angled to see out, the pistol tight in her grip as she waited.

For a while, the only sound she could hear was the blood rushing in her ears, but she held her finger steady on the trigger, ready to shoot the moment his legs moved into view.

Time ticked by. Winter counted the wild beats of her heart, but Kyle didn't head around to the back. No one did.

She was starting to consider her next move when a sound like metal scraping on wood hit her ears. A door being pushed open.

Her breath caught in her throat, and she held it there.

The wood above her creaked. A footstep.

Someone was standing right above her, either Kyle or Troy. Winter swallowed the lump in her throat and clenched her eyes shut as another footstep creaked right above her head. Then she heard the unmistakable sound of a shotgun being pumped.

Winter stiffened, and the gun blasted a huge hole in the deck just above her head. She yelped and rolled.

He knew she was hiding down there, and he was ready to blow holes through his deck until he hit something.

The deck wasn't big enough for her to hope for any kind of a hiding spot. The pistol was slick in her sweaty hands. She had to fire back, and she had to hit her target—because the moment she fired, he'd know exactly where she was.

Winter rolled onto her back, aiming as well as she could from the awkward angle. She could see his shadow through the seams between the porch slats. He pumped the shotgun for a second blast.

Winter squeezed the trigger.

The deck above her trembled and shook as he dropped onto it.

Air burst from her lungs in quick, hot breaths. Deafened by the blast, Winter waited out the ringing in her ears. When her hearing returned, she was met with only silence.

She stayed in that position, watching blood pour between the slats of the deck while listening for the brother she'd hit in the front yard.

Nothing.

Avoiding what had to be a quart of blood pooled two feet away from her head, Winter rolled out from under the deck, cringing in pain as she moved her shoulder. She checked the house, behind her, side to side, and then finally looked at the dead man on the deck with a bullet hole in his chin.

Troy.

She checked all around her once again before taking a cautious step closer to the body. Blood dripped down the wound in her arm. She touched it, and it rolled off her fingertips in perfect spherical droplets, coloring the wet, prickly weeds underfoot. She reached her good hand forward and touched Troy's wrist—which was flung over the edge of the deck—to confirm what she already knew.

No pulse. He was dead. And Mikey was wounded badly enough that he wouldn't be coming after her. That left Dad. Was Kyle Fobb still hunting for her, or had he taken Mikey and fled the scene?

Her gaze trailed back to the glowing red patch of earth near the center of the back lawn. She itched to go check it out but instead took off running for her vehicle.

As she ran, Winter checked the time on her phone—one minute past when she'd told Davenport she would check in. With any luck, he and a swarm of cruisers were on their way to the scene.

32

The EMTs numbed her up with locals, but it still hurt when they squeezed the tiny lead pellets out of her arm and shoulder like fat whiteheads. Once the wounds were clean, they bandaged her up and gave her the obligatory "you should still go to the hospital and get x-rays" speech.

Davenport had arrived less than five minutes after she'd failed to check in, with two other cars in tow. When he saw she was wounded, he called ambulances to the scene, even as she frantically explained what had happened and pointed him toward the man she'd shot who lay unconscious on the front lawn.

Mikey's heartbeat was weak from blood loss. He was taken away in an ambulance to the hospital, but the bullet hadn't penetrated his femoral artery, so he'd likely survive. Troy was dead the moment the bullet went in. Meanwhile, Kyle Fobb and his rusty white truck were long gone.

Winter sat in the back of the ambulance, vaguely watching as Davenport and his officers canvassed the scene. She wondered what they were finding inside the house, but there was no part of her curious enough to go inside. The smell from the porch had told her all she needed to know.

The residence had been set up as a meth lab for quite a while, years it seemed, and the fact that investigators and technicians were all wearing protective gear for the search only enforced that idea. The entire house was toxic. Meth labs always carried a risk of fire and explosions, but the more pressing hazard for investigators were the noxious chemicals used in the manufacturing process.

Even short-term exposure could cause burning eyes, fever, diarrhea, jaundice, hallucinations, chest pain, and any number of other vicious symptoms.

Nasty stuff, and very, very illegal. It was no wonder the occupants of the house had been ready to murder her for simply showing up at the door. And Kyle Fobb had seen her at Lily Ballstow's house, watching her in secret from a distance.

Killers often returned to the scene of their crime, either to relive the high they got from what they had done or to keep an eye on the investigation.

Winter rose to her feet, groaning at the dull ache in her shoulder. But it could've been worse. And though she'd gotten a lot more than she'd bargained for when she went sniffing around this house, there was still one stone left unturned. One she was worried investigators might overlook if she failed to point it out.

Her feet moved sluggishly as she made her way around the side of the house. Retracing her escape route, she bypassed the patch of bloodied grass where Mikey had gone down—now surrounded by tiny markers to outline the spatter and pools. A tech wearing a gas mask and a gray flame-resistant suit crouched on the splintered porch, collecting evidence from the shoot-out that had just taken place.

Deadly force was allowable in cases of self-defense, which this undoubtably had been. Nonetheless, the whole incident promised to be a massive headache involving lots of interviews and paperwork, and it had only just begun.

Still, Winter's gaze was pulled away from the house and across an expansive backyard filled with tall weeds, tiny yellow flowers, and those razor-sharp waist-high thistles. The faint red glow she'd seen before was still there near the middle of the field.

After glancing over her shoulder, she began to pick her way toward it, following a path where the weeds were pushed down, as if somebody frequently walked back and forth to whatever lay at the center of the yard.

Winter stepped up to the red glow and looked down at a circle of wood with metal inlays that closely resembled a manhole cover, but with handles jutting up to pull it open. A well.

Her heart sank, images of Timothy Stewart flashing unbidden through her brain. Repeatedly, over the last few nights, she'd seen him trapped underground, clawing at the walls of a steep ravine. Screaming, being tortured, falling deeper and deeper no matter how she strained to reach for him.

Was he down there? Had Kyle taken Tim?

Winter shook her head, trying to refocus her mind. That was completely illogical. She had seen Tim with her own eyes only yesterday.

Plus, the stench.

Whatever was down there was dead. Beneath the lid of the well was something horrid. No one in her line of work needed to catch a whiff of a decomposing body more than once to remember the odor.

Winter put her fingers to her lips and whistled at two

cops as they made their way toward the back porch. They paused and headed toward her instead.

"Can we get this open?" She pointed at the well with her good arm.

One of the officers was a big guy in his early twenties with a neck so thick it looked like he ate forty-pound dumbbells for breakfast. A crowbar lay nearby, likely used to hook under the handles and lever the cover open, but Schwarzen-copper didn't bother with it. With gloved hands, he and the other cop—who was of normal proportions but looked small next to his partner—yanked the lid open.

The smell punched them all in the face. Rotting meat and stagnant water. Winter turned her head to breathe in fresher air and then turned back to see the cops doing the same.

A warm midafternoon sun shined into the shaft, illuminating smears of red and brown on the stones, but the bottom stayed couched in shadow.

The normal-sized cop took up his flashlight and shined it into the hole. Holding her nose, Winter scooched closer, gasping at what she saw inside.

At the bottom of the pit was a pool of liquid, maybe a foot or so deep. Bones were buoyed all around the perimeter and, at the center, the bloated, putrefied remains of a human body sat slumped. The skin was greenish with patches of red, and a large black worm had burrowed into one eye socket and wiggled in the light.

Instinct forced Winter to pull back and look away. Her stomach lurched with natural disgust. She held it down with a sharp exhale.

"Detective Davenport!" Schwarzen-copper called. "You'd better come look at this. We got a body."

The announcement brought several officers and techs to the well. Collectively, gasps and moans of horror frothed from the crowd as Davenport elbowed his way through to the front.

As he began calling out orders for forensics to excavate every bone out of the hole, Winter turned her face back toward the house and blinked in the sunlight. The combination of the drugs, the comedown from the fight, and the shock of that hideous body were conspiring to steal her breakfast.

"Black?" Davenport stepped up beside her. "You okay?"

"Yeah." She flashed him a quick smile as evidence. "That one just hit me kind of hard for some reason."

He wrinkled his nose in sympathy. "It is certifiably gross."

"How long do you think it's been down there?"

"My guess is a week at least." He spit into the weeds. "Any thoughts on who it might be?"

Winter shook her head. After a few more weeks down that hole, it would've been difficult for anybody but a doctor to say with confidence the decaying body was even human. Like those bones floating around it…forensics was going to have a field day with those.

Davenport shook his head at the ground. "You shouldn't have come here alone."

"Yeah, yeah." She looked at him, but the bright sunlight reflected in his mirrored shades pricked at her eyes, and she had no choice but to drop her gaze to the stickery patches of weeds carpeting the field. She was standing on a patch of sphere-shaped stickers with thorns like knives. Dozens were lodged in the bottom of her shoe.

She was pretty sure he was about to launch into yet another lecture, and she wanted to think about literally anything else, no matter how mundane.

Darnell nodded toward the house. "The whole place is full of evidence. It's going to take weeks to process."

Winter looked up. "More than just a lab?"

"Looks like Kyle Fobb had a pretty diversified portfolio. Along with the meth, about a pound of cocaine has been uncovered so far. I haven't been down to look myself, but one of the techs says she found what looks like magic mushrooms growing in the basement. The Fobb family has a well-established drug ring going on here."

"The home belongs to Kyle's first wife, Faye Anne Diddam. She's in the wind and has been for years. Mikey and Troy had no known addresses. They must've been living here, making drugs for most of their adult lives."

Winter darkened, her shoulders slumping. Troy's life was no more. Killing someone never got easier. Even when she was simply defending herself, it always stayed with her, and she found herself wondering if there was any way she could've made a different choice.

"The paperwork on this SOB's going to take days." Davenport rolled out his shoulders.

"Big ole drug bust. Somebody will get accolades on this thing."

"Probably the mayor." He smiled wryly, his brown eyes peeking over his sunglasses. "But that's fine. I didn't get into this business for glory."

"Why did you?"

"God knows anymore. But I think after this we both deserve a beer."

"Or five." Winter smiled. For the first time since coming to Austin, she felt like she was actually part of a team. But as a cool breeze rushed past her, the feeling dissipated, and her attention drifted back toward the road. "Kyle Fobb's still out there. How could he just leave his sons?"

"Both dead for all he knows."

"I guess we won't be adding Dad of the Year to his long list 'achievements.'"

"Detective Davenport!" A tech jogged closer, a plastic

evidence bag in her hands and her gas mask swinging loosely around her neck. "I think I have an ID on the body."

She lifted the bag so they both could see. Inside was a wallet and Texas state driver's license. The photo was of a man in his early thirties. Blond hair, blue eyes, skinny neck. Below that was a name.

Riley, Nicolas A.

Nick Riley. The man whose complaint against Brent Ballstow had lured Winter into this case in the first place. The same man who had mysteriously gone missing just before Brent and Lily turned up dead.

Winter and Darnell caught each other's gaze, and she knew he saw the connection back to the Ballstows.

Winter turned away from the detective to scan the field, her eyes darting back and forth, searching for shadows of what had happened there. "Nick Riley was already dead when Brent and Lily Ballstow were killed."

"Can't say that for sure yet." Darnell rubbed his forehead with the side of one finger. "But if he was, he definitely didn't kill those two."

Winter pushed her hand through her hair. "What I don't understand is Nick Riley's connection to Kyle Fobb."

"Maybe Brent Ballstow hired Kyle Fobb to kill Nick Riley."

Winter nodded along. The theory had a ring of sense to it. "Lily knew him. He was married to her aunt until a few years ago. Brent probably would've known him too."

"There you go, then. Brent's about to lose his business, but he remembers this scumbag Kyle that he used to know and offers him a bunch of cash to get rid of the problem."

"Then what? Brent doesn't pay up for some reason, so Kyle kills him?" Winter wanted to hear his theory to compare it to her own.

"Why not? It makes sense. Kyle wants to get back at Brent

for stiffing him, so he kills him. Lily walks in on it. He kills her, too, and stages the murder-suicide."

"He recognized me when he saw me at the door. He said he saw me at Lily's house."

Darnell pressed his lips together. "So he's watching the scene after the fact. And then we have Colleen Sturgis, who just so happens to have a connection to Kyle Fobb too. But I don't see how she's involved in any of this."

Winter sighed in frustration. "I'm not quite sure either. But remember when you said Kyle was keeping his nose clean since he got out of prison?"

"Yeah." Darnell shook his head. "This whole operation happening at an ex-con's, and it's all under the radar."

"I don't think he kept a low profile at all. I think Kyle Fobb used his ex-wife's makeup empire to sell drugs. There's a JCH Bloom catalog right on his porch."

"Shit." Darnell actually looked impressed for the first time in a long time.

She knew they were still missing something, overlooking some important connection with Colleen Sturgis. And Brent paying Kyle to kill Nick Riley was speculative at most.

On the brighter side, Darnell now seemed fully convinced that Kyle Fobb was the one they were looking for. No matter the motive, the fact remained that he had killed Nick Riley. Possibly Brent and Lily Ballstow and Colleen Sturgis too. For one reason or another, Kyle Fobb was the connection.

Darnell put out a BOLO on Fobb's truck and an APB on his person. Winter had a feeling that once they had him in custody and under the hot lights, he'd spill everything. That was what they had to hope for anyway.

All they had to go on right now came from one man at the bottom of a well, and he wasn't talking.

33

Noah tossed his suitcase into the back of the car and hurried to the driver's seat. He needed to stay in Lytle to finish his paperwork and to be present for the final briefings. He needed to follow every procedure and take his leave from the FBI on a high note so he'd be welcomed back someday, once he got his head screwed on straight. He needed to show SSA Weston Falkner that he really was a good agent, even if he hadn't been at his best since coming to Austin.

That plan went out the window the second Winter called and told him what had happened. She'd been shot. She said it was fine and even brushed it off, but that hadn't made him feel any better. His wife had been shot, and he needed to be with her now. Everything else could be damned.

As he turned the ignition, a tap on his window startled him. Eve stood there, watching him with a sharp wetness in her eyes that could've been betrayal, or pity, or just dust particles in the air brought up by a dry wind.

Noah rolled down the window. "I'm sorry. I have to go."

"I know." She set her hand on the car door. "Give Winter my best."

"Thank you. I will." He put the car in gear and was about to pull out when he noticed Eve hadn't moved her hand yet.

"If you ever want to get together for a beer or a cookout or whatever, don't hesitate. I would love if you and Winter and me and Jack could get dinner together sometime."

"Yeah. That would be good."

Why the hell was she talking to him about this right now? His wife had just been shot. As much as he liked Eve, the last thing he wanted to do was plan some future happy hour meetup.

"And if you have a case…" Eve continued. "You know, something really personal or important or urgent, and you need somebody in the FBI to help you out with it on a strictly off-the-record basis, please hesitate. Hesitate a lot."

Her words hit him like a bad smell, but he deserved that and worse.

Noah's cheeks puffed out as he exhaled. "I will."

Patting Eve's hand so she finally let go, he peeled out of the parking lot and toward the highway. He had every intention of speeding all the way back to Austin. He needed to be with Winter. Assess the damage and see with his own eyes that she was okay.

He tried to brush it off, but the fact of the matter was she'd gone barreling into the situation with no backup… again. He wanted to give her credit for calling Davenport to follow her in, but she never should've been alone in the first place.

It was his fault for not being at her side. He should've anticipated all these problems when Winter first told him she wanted to go into private practice. Without the rules and procedures of the FBI holding her in place, she was a loose cannon, a vigilante from the comic books. Except this was real life.

"That is a pot and kettle situation." It was something Falkner

would say, and the bastard had a point. Being distracted was dangerous and so was being alone. And as long as they were apart, neither of them could perform at their best. If he was going to spend all his time worrying about Winter anyway, he might as well be at her side, protecting her with a loaded firearm.

If he was there with her in the moment, maybe he could try to persuade her not to leap headfirst into danger quite so enthusiastically or quite as often.

The terrifying truth of it was that he'd almost lost her today. Again. While he was doing paperwork, his wife was being shot at by meth heads who kept dead bodies in their well. The situation was unacceptable.

Noah also knew, though he didn't like to think about it much, that losing her physically was not the only outcome he had to fear. He'd gotten her back after what Justin did to her, yes, but she was a different woman. Different after having been kidnapped, drugged, tortured, and forced to kill an innocent mother and father while their tiny son looked on.

It broke his heart every time she flinched at the sound of a car door shutting. Every time she'd enter a room and immediately press her back against the wall as her eyes darted from one exit to the next. Every time she awoke in a cold sweat after having night terrors about Justin, or more recently about Tim.

Winter had always been guarded and uptight, the effects of trauma suffered in her childhood, but her most recent experience with Justin had switched her into high gear.

She'd lived through so much danger and violence that she was in a constant state of vigilance. Her lizard brain always called for fight or flight, whether she was standing in line for groceries or being shot at. Neither situation seemed inherently more dangerous than the other. They both had equal potential to turn fatal.

Winter was a fighter by nature. So in addition to subconsciously believing anyone anywhere could potentially be trying to kill her, she rushed into truly dangerous situations without thinking or taking proper precaution. Because there were so many times in her past when avoiding violence hadn't been an option, she could no longer discern when nonviolent options were possible.

That was Noah's working theory anyway. From where he was standing, it fit like a glove.

He had promised to be with her in sickness and in health. They were both dealing with a kind of sickness now, the lingering pall of fear that ensured they never felt safe. The sooner he got back to her, the sooner they could begin working through this together.

When he reached the highway, Noah broke away from traffic and pressed the pedal to the floor. He would be at her side soon, and this time, he had no intention of leaving it.

34

Blood poured from my nose, soaking the collar of my undershirt and dotting my hands. I had one hand on the wheel and one clenching my phone as the blood flowed freely. The pain in my head was so intense, like I'd just been struck by a foul ball or the bat that hit it. That woman, that P.I., was a hell of a lot stronger than she looked. Seemed like a cop to me. Even if she wasn't a cop, she definitely knew cops.

In the course of fifteen minutes, everything we'd spent years setting up was destroyed. So many shots had been fired that, even if Troy succeeded in bringing the bitch down, I knew my neighbor must've called the authorities. She had no problem ignoring a single gunshot here and there, but what went down was a Western-style shoot-out.

The cops were going to find the lab, the money, the brochures. I saw their cars in my rearview mirror, and they looked to be racing to the house.

They were going to find Nick down in the well. Would he still be alive when they fished him out? I'd heard him screaming even as I fled the scene. He'd heard the shots, I guessed. He was calling out to the P.I. to save him.

"Help me! I'm down here!"

And my boys…my boys. How could I have left them?

The last ring of the phone registered in my ear as the call went to voicemail.

"Son of a bitch!" I slammed my fist into the dashboard and called again. "Answer me!"

My rusty old truck shook as I hit eighty, my foot like a weight on the pedal. My heart was pounding even louder than the thrum of the engine as everything that had just gone down replayed in my head, over and over.

When last I saw Mikey, he was lying in the grass, bleeding from his knee. I'd tried to get him up, but I couldn't move him. He was delirious, nearly unconscious. I worried he might've already lost too much blood. I couldn't risk bringing him with me. His only hope of surviving the situation was to get caught and taken to the hospital.

Troy told me he knew where she was hiding and went off to go find her. If he did find her and kill her like he said, then maybe he'd gotten away, too, before the cops came. The bike was still parked at the house, gassed up and ready to go. He could be on the road right now or running on foot and not knowing what the hell to do next.

But that woman had a gun. A pistol. All it took was seeing her blast out Mikey's kneecap to know she was a better shot than Troy. I tried to teach him sharpshooting when he was little, like my daddy had taught me, but he never had the patience or the fortitude. His skinny hands shook whenever there was a gun in them.

I hadn't wanted to leave them. I should've stayed and finished the job. I should've gotten both my boys out of there. *What kind of shitty father abandons his sons when some bitch is shooting at them? Leaves his oldest boy bleeding in the dirt...*

I'd done some really messed-up things in my worthless little life, but I'd never abandoned those boys before. Their mother did, up and left all of us when they could barely wipe their own asses without making a mess. Left the home she'd inherited from her father. That was how badly she wanted to be rid of us. She walked right out and never returned. I raised them on my own, making them into what they were today…

My hand shook on the wheel, and my cheeks burned. I shouldn't have left them.

I did it for her, for my boss. And now she wouldn't even answer the damn phone.

Growling with frustration, I called again, and again it rang and rang before clicking over to voicemail.

I was going to her house—that was what I was going to do. She'd told me not to come there, that we couldn't be seen together, that it would ruin the entire operation. But that didn't matter anymore. The operation was already destroyed. No matter what happened, I could never go home again.

If I was lucky and neither of them were dead, then both my boys were currently in police custody. And I knew Mikey would sing like a lark. He never could keep a secret. Even when they were kids and him and Troy would sneak around behind my back, he always confessed as soon as I made him sit down and look into my eyes.

I wagered the boss wouldn't even care that I abandoned my boys to try to warn her. She didn't see everything I'd given up for her, everything I continued to give up so that one day we could be together.

I wondered now if she ever even cared about me. It wasn't the first time I'd wondered that. The whole plan and everything I'd gone through, up to and including leaving my sons to the wolves—had it ever been about us in her mind? I doubted it. All she cared about was herself. I could see that now.

"No!" I punched the steering wheel so hard that something in my hand popped. I liked the pain. I deserved it.

It couldn't be true. She loved me. She'd said so, and a few times she'd even written it down. We were going to be together, come hell or high water.

I was shaking so hard, I had to pull to the side of the road. I ripped the faded red bandanna off my head and used it to stop the blood flowing from my nose.

My thoughts turned to Brent, sitting on his couch late at night watching TV. How normal and comfortable he was in his little suburban cocoon, totally unaware of just how deep his wife had gotten him into the seedy underworld of drugs and makeup. I thought of Lily's eyes, the way she'd looked when the bullet went in right between them.

They were together now, in a way. That seemed appropriate. They'd always been such a loving couple. It was strange, because as individuals, they were scumbags. Yet when you put the two of them together, what you got was unending love and support, the kind of storybook romance that most people could only dream of. It had given me hope that one day my love and I could be just like them.

Maybe we still could. Maybe that was exactly what we deserved.

I jumped when my phone rang. About time.

My thumb clicked the call open. Before I could say a word, she started in—shrill and furious. "What the hell is going on? Why do you keep calling me?"

"It's over."

"What do you mean *it's over*? What's over?"

"This." I broadly indicated the world all around me. "The operation. By tonight, all the drugs will have been confiscated, the lab will be on the news, and we're both going to be wanted criminals."

"What?"

"A P.I. showed up on my doorstep. We ended up getting into a firefight. She shot Mikey." My voice choked. "Oh, god. I don't know if he's okay. And Troy. I left him there with her."

The boss didn't respond right away. I could see her brooding face in my mind—painted lips pursed. "Is the operation secure?"

I coughed out an incredulous laugh. "Did you not hear me? It's over. We are fucked. It's time to take all the money we've been making and get the hell out of the country before it's too late."

"Don't be stupid. We're not going anywhere."

"The cops are going to be all over my house. Do you understand? The product will all be confiscated."

"Then you can just set up shop somewhere else."

I balked, unable to believe what I was hearing. "You don't get it! There's evidence all over the house linking me to you and you to me. We are done. It's over."

"It's not over 'til I say it's over!" Her shriek pierced the line. "This P.I., did you get her name?"

"Yeah. Winter Black of Black Investigations."

I could hear the sound of fingers tapping away on a keyboard. "We're not going anywhere until we get even with Winter Black…" She trailed off. The line was quiet for a moment and then she let out a growl. "Sneaky little bitch. Sam Drewitt, was it?"

"What?"

"Nothing. I'm texting you an address. I want you to meet me there now."

"What address?"

"Winter Black's offices. Get your ass over there now."

"I don't think—"

But like usual, she didn't give a rat's ass about what I thought and hung up before I could get the words out.

I dropped my phone in my lap, onto the blood that had saturated my shirt and pants, and I didn't give a damn. I felt empty inside, broken. She didn't care about my feelings any more than she did my thoughts. All she cared about was getting revenge.

I suppose, if that's what she wants, then I ought to give it to her. When you love someone, you give them everything you have.

But I had so little left to give.

35

Winter sat in her SUV, windows down, across the street from Kyle Fobb's house. The police and technicians were still all over it, combing over a hundred details that would eventually build the case against him and his sons.

She'd given her statement and was cleared to go. Davenport had even offered to have an officer drive her home, but she didn't want to leave her vehicle.

Based on a preliminary assessment, it seemed Nick Riley had sustained a head injury but succumbed to blood loss from a nasty wound that punctured his femoral artery. He likely died the same night he fell or was thrown down the well in Kyle Fobb's backyard.

Winter was glad to know he hadn't suffered any more than that. There were few things she could conceive of that seemed worse than slowly dying of sepsis, dehydration, and exposure while trapped alone in that dark, putrid place.

What she couldn't understand was why Fobb killed him. Unless Darnell's assassin theory panned out, their connection to one another seemed so distant and tenuous. Nick Riley worked for Brent Ballstow, who was married to

Lily, who was the niece of Kyle's ex-wife, Jessica Huberth. Just a few more connections and she'd find Kevin Bacon.

At least the connection to Colleen Sturgis was straightforward—he was her dealer. But drug dealers didn't usually go around killing their clients for no reason. It was bad business. Maybe if Sturgis owed him a debt, but that seemed rather far-fetched, given how much money that woman seemed to be swimming in. Plus, she fronted Jessica Huberth the money to start the MLM to funnel makeup and drugs.

All Winter really had to go on—the wild card that had her stumped—was the JCH Bloom catalog she'd found in Lily's trash can.

It was possible Lily got Kyle's address from Colleen. She and Kyle had known each other since middle school. Maybe Lily and Brent hired Kyle to kill Nick…but instead of paying him to do the job, they threatened to expose his drug operation to the police. So he killed them.

But Jessica Huberth was the face of the company that was funneling the drugs. The more Winter thought about it, the more it made sense that the store clerk Amy Powell and Jessica's daughter Sybil were the dealers. And Lily was, too, back when she was alive. Kyle made the product.

Winter dug through a pile of papers sitting on the passenger seat beside her until she found the JCH Bloom catalog. Even after all this time, it still held the faintest hint of an ethereal red glow. She looked at the address on the back. Only five numbers, but something about the flourish and the medium told her it was written by a woman. By Lily, not Brent.

She opened to the inside of the front cover to find a letter from the editor—yet another attempt to make the publication seem less like an advertisement and more like a magazine. Framed in a pretty floral border was a picture of the founder, Jessica Huberth, her dark-chocolate hair in small victory curls and a big, open-mouthed, *look at me laughing* smile on her face.

Feminine romanticism is in this spring, the letter read. *Ignite your inner princess and find your Prince Charming with our new range of hand-selected products!*

Winter skimmed the letter. Blah, blah, blah, *makeup tutorials*. Blah, blah, blah, *interviews with industry leaders*.

Introducing "Beauty Beyond the Surface," where we delve into the emotional aspects of beauty, fostering self-love and acceptance. Embrace your uniqueness and let makeup and haircare become your canvas for romantic self-expression.

Warmest wishes—blah, blah, blah. *Jessica Huberth, Editor-in-Chief.*

Jessica Huberth was calling all the shots. Taking down Kyle meant taking down her operation. And Kyle Fobb wasn't just cooking drugs for her. He was killing people.

Why would an ex-con ex-husband risk more jail time, including the death penalty, for his ex-wife?

Winter threw the catalog down onto the passenger seat. The answer to that question was as old as time and what all great tragedies were built on. Kyle was still in love with her.

Buckling up carefully so as not to hurt her shoulder further, she put the key in the ignition, and took off.

There was nobody better at research than her perky office assistant, and Winter had some new questions boiling in her brain that needed answering.

As she headed back into town, she thought more and more about the idea of Jessica calling the shots.

Lily and Brent's home was not broken into. Nor was Colleen's. Which meant someone had a key. Maybe Aunt Jessica had a spare key to Lily's house. Cara Criver of Ballstow's Appliances told her that Lily had lost her key. Winter smacked the steering wheel. Because Jessica took it.

And maybe Jesssica somehow stole one of Colleen's keys too.

Winter was just a few blocks from her office when the phone rang over the speaker system. "Ariel, hi, I'm almost to the office."

"Not Ariel, but your timing is perfect."

On instinct, Winter double-checked the display number. "Who is this?"

"Shut your mouth and listen to me." The angry voice was familiar. "I have your pretty little assistant, and I'm going to blow her cute little butt off if you don't get here in the next two minutes."

Winter knew that idiolect. The woman with the chocolate curls who told her to sell her *cute little butt off*. The business mogul. The ex-wife. Jessica Huberth. And the mastermind behind all this.

Winter straightened in her seat as if hit by a jolt of electricity. Her phone buzzed on the passenger seat. A text had come in from Ariel's phone. A photo.

Veering the Pilot onto the shoulder, Winter opened the image. A picture of her own office—the break room and kitchen behind the new bookshelves—the only part of the office that could never be seen from the street. Ariel was on her knees on the hardwood, gagged and tied up with white nylon cord. Black streaks of mascara ran down from both eyes.

"Don't hurt her, Jessica." Winter spoke quickly. "Tell me what you want."

"I want you, *Winter Black*. Just you. We have a lot to discuss. And I want you now, or I'm going to cut off her little toe."

Winter narrowed her eyes. "Is Kyle with you?" She needed to know what she was up against.

"No questions. Just get here right now. Oh, and by the way, if I see a cop, she's dead." She hung up.

Winter was now more convinced than ever that Kyle Fobb was just her obsequious flunky with the world's worst case of unrequited love—because Jessica Huberth clearly did not care what happened to him.

And now, because Kyle Fobb had been exposed, it was only a matter of time before Jessica Huberth was too.

Winter called Davenport to tell him what was happening, even though something told her Huberth wasn't lying when she threatened to hurt Ariel. It went to the same voicemail as before.

After the beep, she left a message, explaining the details of the hostage situation as fast as she could. Then, as she pulled onto the road to get to the office in two minutes' time, she called the only person she wanted to see right now.

He answered after the first ring. "Hey, darlin'. How you doin'?

"I need you to meet me at my office as quick as you can."

"I'm on the highway now, maybe ten minutes off. What's going on? Are you okay?"

Winter tried to take a breath to calm herself, but her heart was beating so hard, it shot the air from her lungs in hard bursts. "The killer has Ariel."

36

I paced behind the woman we'd bound and gagged.

When I pulled up to the place, Jessica had been waiting outside. She'd sent me in first to take the woman captive and secure the area. Only after all that was done did she waltz in like a queen and start barking out orders.

I felt numb. And I didn't understand any part of Jessica's new plan. Usually, she was so methodical, so cold. Then again, this wasn't the first time I'd seen her lose her temper and run hot. Right now, she was so furious that the tips of her ears had gone red.

After threatening the P.I., Jessica hung up the phone and smacked it down on the little oval-shaped table at the center of the room.

"What are we doing here?" I kept my eyes on the floor underfoot. It looked like it had just been refinished—shiny and clean. I was getting my filthy boot prints all over it. Back and forth, I couldn't stop. Evidence all over the place. "This doesn't make any sense."

"Shut up!" Jessica balled her snow-white hands into fists.

"The last thing I need right now is more of your stupid questions."

I bit my lip, but I just couldn't keep it in. "She's going to bring the cops."

Jessica glared at me before turning her hate to the tied-up receptionist. "I told her what would happen if she did."

"Whoop de shit! She's still gonna bring the cops. And then what, huh? We've got a hostage. Best case, you kill the P.I. and this bitch, and then you and me get to spend the rest of our lives in prison."

"I'm not going to kill them, you idiot." Jessica walked up to me and grabbed my wrist. I warmed at her touch, every part of me longing for her now. When she slapped the cold gun into my hand, I went numb. "You're going to kill them."

I looked behind me at the sobbing young woman. "But there's no reason. I need a reason."

"The reason is I told you to."

"Let's just go, Jess." I took her hand in mine. "Forget about the P.I. She doesn't matter."

With a look of disgust, Jessica yanked it away. "Doesn't matter? She ruined everything! You think I'm just going to sit by and stand for it? Let that pasty bitch get the best of me?" A cold laugh trickled past her teeth as she pointed at the receptionist. "Watch her. I'm going to keep an eye on the door."

Jessica checked her watch before turning on her high heel to stride out of the room with her head held high. To me, it felt like she took all the energy in the room with her. The moment she was gone, I no longer needed to pace. Instead, I slumped into a chair at the table.

"It's all shit now." I ran my fingers back and forth across the glass, leaving about a hundred fingerprints. What did I care anymore?

This was supposed to be easy—a way for me to distribute quantity without having to deal with cartels, or gangs, or even standard racoon-faced dealers. Me and the boys just had to worry about manufacturing the goods, and Jessica managed Amy, Lily, Sybil, and the other girls that sold the shit to Colleen's friends and friends of friends. Jessica laundered the money through JCH Bloom. Everybody made money. Everybody won. Every time.

But when Lily's gorilla of a husband was caught manhandling his employees—again—the Ballstows faced losing everything. Lily had dozens of creditors on her ass, both legitimate and criminal. They needed money fast. Lily decided to find out where the drugs were coming from and threaten to blackmail Jessica and expose the connection.

Jessica kept Lily and everybody else in the dark about where the drugs came from. I scrubbed my hand over my face, ignoring the whimpers of the tied-up secretary. That was why we'd spent the last few years basically pretending like we never spoke. The less the girls knew about the inner workings of the scheme, the better.

I never understood why Colleen pointed her my way. Colleen had money and drugs. She didn't need anything from Lily. But because of Colleen, Lily found out that Jessica and I never lost contact after our divorce. She found out where the drugs were being manufactured. She found out everything. And that smug bitch went to her Aunt Jessica and demanded a payoff to keep her mouth shut.

Jessica had no intention of giving Lily one red cent. But because Lily was her niece, Jessica offered an alternative, promising to put the fear of God in Nick to get him to drop the lawsuit.

That was when Jessica called me, the fixer, to do just that. She said Lily would give up on the blackmail if this lawsuit against Ballstow's Appliances was dropped. I wasn't supposed to kill him. There was no reason to kill him. But he hadn't seen that well in the ground when he was trying to escape from me.

I wondered how different everything might've been if Troy had just closed the damn cover after tossing the bones from the hunt in it.

Nick would've dropped the suit, and maybe Lily would've been so relieved that she would've apologized to us for threatening us in the first place.

Happy ending.

But no.

Nick had to go and fall down the well.

Then I told Jessica about it, and she thought that meant Nick was dead. Then she told Lily, who turned around and blackmailed us even more. Over the meth lab location and murder!

At that point, Lily deserved to die, because really, what was the alternative?

And Brent had to go, too, because we had to make it look realistic.

And Colleen…she was really stupid. Her betrayal alone was reason enough to kill her. That was what Jessica said, and that Colleen must realize we'd killed Lily and Brent, and so I had to kill her too. I swallowed hard, my mouth sour. I could still feel a hunk of roast beef wedged in my teeth from that sandwich.

I couldn't get any of them out of my head. And now my sons were up there, too, haunting me.

Back when Jessica told me that I had to kill her niece, her voice had been so normal, so unremarkable. Like asking for a fancy coffee drink. And she was the boss, so I did it. I didn't personally give a damn about Lily or her husband. But it needled me, how easy it was for Jessica to order a hit on her own family, even with Lily and all her blackmailing. I mean, we could've just given her some money. We'd made a lot in a very short time.

We were family, too, Jessica and me. Or at least, that was what she always told me. Even if she didn't seem to care that I'd been shot at earlier today. That my nose was broken and still oozing blood. Or that both my sons might be dead.

"My sons…" Tears sprang to my eyes. I tried to hold them back, but the pain in my chest was too much. I leaned on my elbows, lurching over the table.

I never meant to hurt them. I'd wanted to make money for them, too, so they could look after themselves. But I shouldn't have brought them in on this in the first place.

This was never supposed to be a permanent business. When Jessica asked me to help her get the start-up capital from Colleen, she pitched it as a temporary scheme. A way to make a lot of money so we could get away together. Grow the business fast and then move to Costa Rica.

We'd buy a house, hang out on the beaches, and never think about money or drugs ever again. Our lives could be paradise, so long as we were patient. We just had to wait for the right time, she always said.

That time was right now. We needed to run. I wanted to trust Jessica, like I always had. She was smarter than me, better at all this stuff. I was just a grunt, a run-of-the-mill scumbag from the streets. It was what I'd always been. But I thought somehow that she saw more.

I'd always felt so lucky that somebody like Jessica could love someone like me. She saw something in me nobody else ever had. She trusted me with cooking drugs, with scaring people, and killing them too. That had to mean she believed in me.

But now I doubted that was ever true. Maybe she was just using me. Maybe she always had been.

I looked at the gun in my hand, felt its solemn weight. If

she was just using me like a grunt, there was no reason to stick around to do her dirty work. The time to act was now, and if that meant I had to cut ties and move on, so be it.

It was going to be messy, though. If my divorce was proof of anything, it was that there was only one way to cut ties with a woman as devious as Jessica Huberth.

37

Winter parallel parked in front of Peek-a-Brew Café, a popular coffee shop down the street from her office. After securing her .38 in the inside pocket of a jacket she'd had in her vehicle, she got out, the holes in her shoulder and neck screaming for mercy. The localized analgesics had worn off, giving her the wherewithal to drive and shoot and do anything else that might be necessary.

The flipside was that meant the pain was back with a stinging, angry vengeance. She was hit with bird shot, so the pain was greater than the internal damage it caused, but that arm wasn't going to be good for much of anything for the next few days.

She kept the gun in her hand hidden inside her jacket, so as not to spook any passersby, and made her way toward the office. The roll-down coverings on the front-facing window were all drawn, and the *Closed* sign had been hung on the knob. As she approached, she could peer through cracks in the darkened rolling blinds.

She usually only ever rolled the blinds down when they closed for the night, making it even more eerie to see it like that during the day. Even the shade over the door had been pulled. Through tiny cracks in the fabric, she could see that all the lights were off.

Winter's heart pounded in rhythm with the pain in her shoulder. It was a trap. She knew it was a trap. All the way over, she'd been trying to suss out what she could possibly have that Kyle and Jessica would want, and unfortunately, there was only one answer.

Revenge. She didn't have anything they needed. No material evidence they could potentially steal and abscond with. If they were smart, they'd be in a car right now, hightailing it to Mexico. Instead, they were in her office tormenting her assistant, using her as bait to lure Winter to them.

They wanted to hurt her, nothing more. Together, they'd already killed Jessica's niece and her husband and Kyle's childhood friend. The man had even fled the scene at his own house, leaving his grown sons bleeding and dying. Neither of them had a conscience.

It didn't help her nerves that Kyle Fobb appeared to be a sharpshooter. The second she opened the door, he could bury a bullet between her eyes just like he'd done with Lily. She wouldn't even get a chance to react or defend herself. Maybe Mexico was in their plans after all, and they just wanted to deal with Winter first.

She did not want to go in there. Every instinct in her body—every innately animalistic part of her—was urging her to turn tail and run. Get away. Stay alive. But she could never do that. Ariel was in danger. Tied up, terrified. And with at least one psycho waving a gun in her face.

The whole situation was Winter's fault. Her insatiable curiosity had put them right in the middle of it once again. Part of her wished she'd listened to Noah and Davenport and let sleeping dogs lie. But if she had, none of the victims ever would've gotten justice.

Even if she somehow managed to get through this—and she had to believe she could—Ariel might never want to come back to work after this. Black Investigations was not turning out to be the best employer. Long nights, leaky toilets, and crazed drug dealers kidnapping employees.

Winter hadn't even settled on a retirement plan yet.

With a heavy gulp, she set her hand on the office door. She knew the longer she hesitated, the harder this was going to be. So she turned the knob, let the door swing open, and stepped inside.

"If it isn't Sam Drewitt."

Winter looked toward the cold voice. Jessica Huberth sat behind Ariel's desk with her elbows propped on top and her fingers tented. Her curls were a bit frizzy and askew, but her makeup was still impeccable. Sunlight peeked through the cracks in the blinds, bathing the office in bars of light and shadow.

Winter had never seen the place look like this before. She felt like she'd just stepped into a cage.

"Shut the door," Jessica ordered.

The last thing she wanted was to shut that door. She needed to get to Ariel and get her out before either of them got shot, but she was nowhere to be seen. In the picture, she had been tied up in the break room, just beyond the curve of the bookcase.

"Take it easy." Winter pressed the door closed just shy of hearing the click that indicated the bolt had gone into the strike plate. Then she hazarded a cautious step closer to the desk. "You don't want to do anything you might regret."

"Four years. It took me four years and almost a million dollars to build JCH Bloom into the company that it's become. And in one day, you completely destroyed it."

"Good thing that million belonged to Colleen." Winter's thumb stroked the gun in her hand, hidden under her jacket. "How did you get her to put up the cash anyway?"

Jessica shrugged her petite shoulders. "Kyle threatened to expose her past and her lifestyle to all her new friends. The *nouveaux riches* are incredibly easy to blackmail."

"I guess Lily got that same impression." Winter took another step.

To face Jessica sitting at Ariel's desk, she had to turn her back on the entrance, which she did not want to do. Instead, she approached in a half circle, so the woman would not be staring directly at the door over Winter's shoulder.

"Don't talk to me about Lily."

"She was your niece. How could you?"

"How could she!" Jessica leaped to her feet and slammed her open palm on the desk.

Winter startled and stopped in her tracks.

"I gave her a job with unlimited earning potential, and then she had the nerve to try to blackmail me. Even after I took care of Nick for her! That bitch got what she deserved."

"Speaking of, did Nick Riley get what he deserved?"

She waved a dismissive hand like swatting at a fly. "I thought if I got him to drop the suit, Lily would realize what a big mistake she'd made. I never told Kyle to kill him. But what can you expect when working with a dumb animal? You get what you get."

"The suit would've been dropped with Nick dead. So why did you still have Lily and Brent killed?"

As Jessica lifted her face, a stream of light illuminated her eyes and lips. Winter could see every wrinkle under her makeup, the aging face she fought so hard to keep hidden.

"Because Lily, that greedy, ungrateful little bitch, wanted money anyway! She had drugs and murder hanging over us. So she had to go, along with her useless husband." Jessica's mouth pinched into a tight little knot. "And of course, dumb Colleen with her dumb fried brain was the idiot who told Lily about the location of Kyle's drug operation for JCH Bloom in the first place. Who does that? Kyle did the world a favor that day!"

"And what about Kyle? Where does he fit into all this?"

"Oh, I think you know the answer to that."

The door beyond the bookshelves swung open, and Kyle stepped into the room, a huge pistol—probably a Desert Eagle—in his grip. A single shot to the head with that thing wasn't going to leave a tiny hole like the 9mm that killed Lily. She'd have an exit hole in her head the size of a baseball.

Winter turned her attention back to Jessica. "You don't want to do this."

"Oh, I definitely do. Nobody ruins my business and gets away with it." The small woman angled her head toward Kyle. "Do it. Finish her."

38

"Wait!" Winter put out her empty hand like a shield. "There's still one thing I don't understand."

Jessica's gaze went to Kyle, micro-expressions waving across her perfectly plucked eyebrows. Winter couldn't interpret them, but Kyle nodded and lowered his gun by an inch.

"I get it now. Your business model. It's brilliant, actually. You've figured out how to bypass all the organized crime that'd try to muscle in on you by selling only to select clientele."

"Only the best." Jessica pulled a self-satisfied smile that gave Winter hope. Like she had anticipated, Little Miss Self-Styled Celebrity had an ego the size of a football stadium. Maybe if she could just keep her talking and distracted, Noah could get here in time.

"Colleen set up the drug meets with her rich friends, and you sent in your girls. I bet you packaged the drugs all pretty and presented them with a real salon experience."

Jessica smiled even more and set a finger to her chin. "Like the Silver Tier package you went home with, we offered product samples, easy reordering, and subscription services. All very sophisticated."

"It makes sense why you felt Lily had to die." Winter nodded sympathetically. "She was going to expose your whole business. And you had to kill Brent with her, or he might become a problem. And Colleen betrayed you. But she was your biggest client, and Lily was one of your top earners. How did you plan to carry on the business without them?"

"Do you honestly think I'm stupid enough to have four people murdered and then not leave town?"

Winter was pretty sure she wasn't supposed to answer that.

"I never planned on running this business until I was in my grave. Lily doing what she did just forced me to move my exit plans up a little. I have more money than I know what to do with. It's time to cut ties here and get out of Austin."

Kyle's eyes softened gently as she spoke. He wasn't looking at Winter anymore, though his gun was still pointed at her chest. The look on his face was unmistakable. He was in love with Jessica. But she hadn't once even glanced in his direction.

"Where will you go?" Winter asked.

"Far away from here. Away from Austin and the stink of the drug trade and everyone associated with it."

Kyle took a step forward. His eyes looked hazy and cloudy. Could those be tears?

His gaze snapped to Winter. "My sons. Are they dead? Did you kill them?"

Her heart leaped into her throat. She really didn't want to answer that. He lifted the gun and steadied his aim between her eyes. Her throat felt like it was swelling shut. She swallowed. "Mikey was rushed to the hospital. He'll be okay. But Troy…"

Kyle Fobb's jaw tightened, skin growing ashy in waves.

His eyes wandered listlessly across the room as the gun in his hand dipped toward the floor.

Winter felt his pain like a punch to her ribs. She hadn't wanted to kill anybody, but in that moment, it had been either him or her.

"One less loose end to worry about." Jessica's expression was flat, wiped of emotion, like an ornate Venetian mask. She turned from Kyle to Winter. "Now you're the only thing standing in the way of my future. Once you and the little bitch in the back are dead, I can leave this all behind and go enjoy the money I earned. The money I deserve."

She stepped out from behind the desk, her impossibly high heels clicking on the hardwood, and set a hand on her hip. "Finish her, Kyle."

His chest heaved with every breath as he hesitated. Kyle raised his downcast eyes. Then he raised his gun.

Winter drew her own weapon and aimed, but not before Kyle pulled the trigger.

39

I wasn't ready for how violently the shot would toss her body around. Her back hit the desk and she lay slumped, her spine arched in a backbend over it. Her beautiful face had a hole right through it—her nose and eyes were gone. The exit wound had smashed the back of her skull to pieces. Splinters of bone and globs of brain splattered the desk and the wall behind her.

My hearing faded in and out with high-pitched ringing. I blinked, half expecting the horrible image to vanish like nightmares did by dawn. If anything, blinking made it worse. I drew closer, stumbling. The gun felt so heavy in my hand, but I held tight to it. If I dropped it, I would collapse too. My knees had never felt so shaky.

"Jessica…"

Saying her name cast a spell over my surroundings, and time stood still. When we started up the drug ring, she told me to call her *Boss* so nobody would suspect anything or figure out our connection. I should've known then. No woman who loved me would ever forbid me from speaking her name. Whenever she said mine, my heart would sing and take flight.

I was so stupid. I shook my head and took a calculated inhalation.

The black-haired P.I., Winter Black, stared with her mouth agape, a pistol in her hands pointed right at me. She looked like she was catching her breath, too, but from shouting at me, I think. In the aftermath of the gun blast, I hadn't heard a word.

"Kyle…" She stood taller. "Please, put the gun down. We can talk about this."

The tears fogging my eyes raced down my cheeks, burning like acid. Troy was dead. Mikey was probably dying. And Jessica didn't care. Their own mother had been nothing but a disappointment—a junkie who loved drugs more than anything else.

Jessica was a junkie too. I could see that now. Only her drugs of choice were money and power. The way she got her fix was using her money to wield power over others.

"My boys." I blinked. More tears. "She never cared about them at all. She never cared about me." I sniffed and wiped my nose with my arm.

"I'm sorry." Black's voice was soft, but her gun didn't waver.

"She always treated my sons like they were nothing. Ignored them, complained to me that they were too needy, longing for a mother's gentle touch. It was no different from how she treated her own daughter. Little Sybil, all decked out and pushing drugs for her mother. That's the only reason Boss ever showed her any attention. Boss…"

A sad laugh let loose from deep inside. I was still calling her boss. I was so pathetic.

I raised my free hand to my temple, rocking back and forth. "Oh, god. What have I done?"

"Kyle. It's gonna be okay." Black took a tenuous step toward me, but I raised the barrel and stopped her in place. I refused to walk into Winter's snare.

"This is your fault! If you just minded your own business, this never would've happened." It was a standoff. But my Desert Eagle was bigger. And I was a great shot—my one and only skill.

I wanted to kill her then. Kill her and any other cop that showed up. Jessica was dead. Nothing else mattered now...

But the gun felt so heavy in my hand. And the truth was, I didn't care enough to kill her. I hadn't wanted to kill anyone. I wasn't a murderer. Just a dumb, lonely guy in love.

My hand dropped to my side, and I looked again at Jessica. With her eyes basically blown out now, her brain was on full display, a pile of jelly framed by those pristine curls. It was weird, though, because her natural scowl was gone. In a way, she looked happy to see me for the first time ever.

"I had hoped that maybe someday, somehow..." My voice choked. "If I worked hard enough, you know?" I looked at Black, and she nodded. "Sacrificed everything. I really believed one day she'd love me as much as I loved her."

She lowered her weapon several inches. "That isn't your fault, Kyle."

"I made excuses for her. I ignored how she treated everyone else..." Hearing those words come out of my mouth made me feel even stupider. "It was always her plan to toss me away. I was part of the filthy drug trade she needed but thought she was too good for. I was the stink she was going to wash off and forget about once she had enough money."

"I'm sorry." Black looked like she actually meant it when she said those words again.

All Jessica's promises were just lies used to manipulate me like she manipulated everybody else. "I wasted my whole life and the lives of both my children on a woman who could never love any of us."

"Kyle, this is not your fault."

"Troy's dead." He was abandoned by his father, just like he'd been abandoned by his mother years before. "And Mikey's lying in a hospital somewhere, wondering what happened to me." The pain in my heart was too much to take. I gripped the skin on my chest with my free hand, tore at it with my grubby nails.

"We can find out where Mikey is."

"But I left them. For her, always for her. This was my fault. I killed my boys."

"No, you didn't."

"I let Jessica kill my boys!"

She didn't argue that point.

"I'm so stupid!" The words hurt like needles to my brain. That devious bitch was still torturing me. It would never stop.

"Kyle, Kyle…" Black was saying my name again and again. But nothing she said could change anything. "Mikey is still alive. Put the gun down, and I can take you to see him."

"Mikey?" My heart skipped a beat. I blinked and wiped the snot and blood from my upper lip on my forearm again.

"Yes. He's alive. He's going to be okay. But he needs you. Put the gun down."

I looked at her gun and then down at mine. It was so unbearably heavy in my tired hand.

The front door must've opened, though I didn't hear it. But I sensed something, which caused me to look back up and snap my head in that direction.

A man had come in, big and burly, wearing an FBI windbreaker. His gun was drawn and pointed at me, and he was suddenly standing at Black's side. How the fuck had he gotten in? I was really losing it.

"Drop the gun," the big guy ordered in a deep voice.

I sniffled and looked back at Jessica's bloody face, seeking guidance. I was so used to taking her orders. Love, hate, and hopelessness swirled like a tornado inside me.

She'd been a goddess in my eyes. But just like everybody else, it only took one bullet to bury her. She wasn't so special after all. And I had to be punished, too, for wasting my life worshipping her.

The gun trembled in my hand.

"Jessica's gone. Troy. Everything's gone." I'd never felt such pain, such pressure growing in my chest. Was I having a heart attack? "I killed Brent, Lily, Colleen. Nick. He's still down in my well, by the way. You should probably go get him out." I looked at Black.

"Kyle, he's gone. He died the night he fell down there."

"No." I pressed a hand to my face. I couldn't breathe. "I heard him earlier. And every night, I…"

I could hear Nick screaming in my ears right now, just as plainly as I could taste that strange roast beef sandwich. I saw Lily, her eyes wide as the bullet that went into her brain. I felt the heat of Brent's hand in mine as I pressed the barrel to the side of his head and squeezed the trigger.

I saw Colleen, a floating island in a pool of blood.

They were all dead. Four people dead because Jessica told me to kill them. I followed her orders like a brainwashed attack dog. I killed for her again, and again, and again. And still, I wasn't good enough.

Help me! The screams echoed off the stone walls of my mind and deep into my guts. *Please! Help me!*

But now, it wasn't Nick's voice. It was my own, screaming into the void. Begging for mercy from God, though I had long ago turned my back on him.

The man ordered me to drop the gun again.

Black talked again about Mikey in the hospital.

I couldn't really understand any of it.

The gun, too heavy to hold up, dangled from my fingertips as I moved closer to Jessica.

"She's the only woman I ever loved." I touched her hair, gathering blood on my fingertips. Then I wiped my hand over my face to feel her warmth one last time. "Maybe now we can finally be happy together."

I lifted the gun and pressed the barrel under my chin. It was still warm. Warmer than Jessica's embrace had ever been.

"Kyle, no!" Black screamed as I fired.

40

Noah turned his head as blood and gore sprayed from the man's shattered skull.

At his side, Winter choked out a sob and grabbed his bicep, her body curling into his. He put his arm around her and drew her close.

He looked back up as the body hit the floor with a lifeless *thunk*. For a few seconds that stretched on forever, neither of them moved or said a word. No matter how many times he'd seen people die, he'd never get used to it. The scent of blood and gunpowder trickled into his nostrils like smelling salts.

Gripping Winter's uninjured shoulder, Noah turned to face her directly. "Are you all right?"

Her piercing blue eyes were so wide, so filled with dread. She put her head back on his chest with a nod. "I'm fine."

He hugged her tight, making sure she really was there and really was intact.

Abruptly, Winter pulled back. "Ariel." She rushed past him and into the break room in the back.

Noah took out his phone and called the police, relaying what little he knew of what had happened. Two bodies lay before him, devastated by the high caliber rounds of a Desert Eagle, in what he could only assume had been an actual murder-suicide.

The same way this whole thing had started.

As he got off the phone, he locked the front door, turning around as Winter staggered out of the back with Ariel, her arm slung around her shoulder. Winter shielded Ariel from having to see the carnage, holding a hand next to her eyes and pulling her head into her shoulder like she might do a child.

Noah could see a few pale-gray bruises coloring Ariel's jawline. Her bottom lip was bleeding, her hair and clothes were in disarray, and she had been crying, but otherwise, she seemed unharmed.

Noah hurried to Ariel's other side. They walked past the bodies of Jessica Huberth and Kyle Fobb and into Winter's office—the only place they could all avoid having to look at them.

They helped Ariel to a seat on the small couch. Noah went to each of the glass walls and drew the blinds as Winter crouched in front of the young woman and took her by the hand. Then Noah headed into the back and fetched a few bottles of water from the fridge.

In his personal experience, the best thing to do when anybody suffered any kind of emotional trauma was to offer them something to drink. It always helped, though he wasn't sure exactly why. They often didn't drink it, but it gave them something to hold, something to fiddle with, something to ground them in the moment. Warm drinks were best, but water worked too.

Noah handed Ariel the bottle. "Is there any bodily harm that you know of? Possible internal injuries?"

"No, she just smacked me across the face a few times after they tied me up. I'll be okay." Ariel took the water but didn't open it. "I'm so sorry, Winter." She buried her face in her hands, sobbing quietly.

"This is not your fault."

"Well, I was busy on the phone, distracted by the toilet, and Kyle just walked right in. I looked up and asked how I could help him. Just like that. I didn't even really look at him, though." She scoffed and shook her head in disgust. "How much time have I spent researching him, and I still didn't recognize the guy?"

"It's not always easy to recognize people out of context, especially when you aren't expecting them. Besides, Kyle was looking a lot more haggard than he did in any of his old pictures."

Noah glanced out into the hall at the body of the broken man lying prone on the hardwood. The pool of blood was spreading slowly, now touching the seating area. He pulled the door a bit more closed, leaving a crack so he could hear when the authorities arrived.

"I should've been on guard." Ariel fiddled with the plastic cap on her water bottle. "I wasn't paying attention, and I nearly got everyone killed."

"This is not your fault, Ariel…" Winter trailed off as her gaze flicked to Noah. Then she sighed and pulled herself up from a crouch to sit at Ariel's side. "But this is the job. When you're working with criminals, you can never expect to be one hundred percent safe."

"I know that—"

"Listen, I love having you here." Winter touched Ariel's arm. "Your research skills are off the charts, and you have the potential to be an amazing detective. But this job is not for everyone. If you want to be a detective someday, it'll take a lot of hard work and dedication…and getting comfortable with a situation going off the rails at a moment's notice. Just like working as a police officer, this job is eighty percent boredom and paperwork, ten percent action, and ten percent wondering what the hell just happened."

Ariel nodded, her face turned toward her knees. "Wow, I never thought of it that way."

Noah and Winter shared a knowing look.

"Don't give me an answer right now." Winter set a hand on her shoulder. "I want you to stay but can't always be here to protect you. At some point, you'll have to learn how to protect yourself. If you want to stay on, we'll look into getting you enrolled in self-defense classes."

The sound of a commotion near the front door caught Noah's attention.

Meeting his gaze, Winter rose to her feet. Leaving Ariel on the couch, they walked out into the main office together.

Noah unlocked the door, and a few uniforms filtered into the room, followed by Detective Davenport. When he pulled off his sunglasses, the bags under his eyes suggested he hadn't had a good night's sleep since Lily and Brent Ballstow turned up dead. Noah couldn't help feeling a pang of empathy for the man. All the same, he had no desire to switch places with him.

"Holy…" was all Davenport said, before looking at Winter and shaking his head. "What the hell happened?"

"Kyle Fobb was our killer." Winter stepped up to his side. "He confessed to killing Nick Riley and Brent and Lily Ballstow. And Colleen Sturgis. But Jessica Huberth, the CEO of JCH Bloom, was the one pulling all the strings. She's the one sprawled across the front desk right there."

"Who pulled the trigger here?"

"Fobb did." Her voice choked, and she cleared her throat. "I guess he finally got tired of being her puppet."

"Silly me, I thought you might've been heading home to sleep off your bullet wound."

"It was bird shot. And I was. Well, I was on my way here

and then home." Winter rolled out her shoulder. "And that's when they called from Ariel's phone. They had my assistant held hostage at gunpoint. Said I had two minutes to get here, and if I informed the police, she was as good as dead."

"Black…" He shook his head.

Noah felt the man's pain now more than ever. But it was a step in the right direction, Winter contacting them both. He hoped Davenport would come to that conclusion too.

"I just wish you'd have waited for us. Or called 911 when you got my voicemail."

"They weren't messing around. And I knew it. Instinct. I mean, look at this scene. You can't tell me my instincts weren't dead on." Under her breath, she added, "They would've killed my assistant without blinking. And you respond to my messages. I mean, here you are for the second time today."

Noah stepped up to her side and set his hand lightly on the small of her back. "She did call for backup, Darnell. And she hadn't shut the door all the way, so I could enter unnoticed at the right moment."

He was never more grateful they were so in sync. Would the police have noticed that? He doubted it.

Davenport snorted his agreement while shaking his head at the scene a second time. "Fair enough. I think you deserve more than a few beers at this point. Maybe some shots of whiskey."

"Maybe." Her cheek pulled with a tired half smile as she turned to Noah. "All I really want is a bath tonight, though. With you in it."

41

That night, Winter didn't have any dreams. She awoke alone in bed when the sun was already high enough in the sky that she couldn't see it through her east-facing window. The smell of coffee and bacon lingered in the air. Her shoulder was so stiff, though. So for a long time, she lay there, just staring at the ceiling.

She thought about Tim, but only to acknowledge just how happy she was not to spend the entire night watching him be tortured by monsters and the flames of hell. How long would it last? She didn't know.

But maybe, just maybe, the nightmares were finally over.

When Winter rose from bed, she did her morning ablutions and got herself a cup of coffee. Then she spotted Noah sitting out on the front porch in one of their wooden Adirondack chairs. She fixed herself a plate of bacon and eggs—still warm on the stove—and went out to join him.

The wood creaked under her bare feet.

Noah looked up at her and smiled. "There she is. I was wondering when you'd get up."

She gave him a peck on the lips, settled into the chair next to him, and crunched on a piece of bacon.

It was perfect—crispy and soft in all the right places. She ate the whole piece without coming up for air.

"Ariel called." Noah sipped his coffee. "She didn't want to wake you, so she called me. She wants to take a few days off to recover."

"Does that mean she'll be coming back to work?"

He shrugged. "I assume so."

Winter brought another slice to her lips, then lowered it with a sigh. "Do you think I was too hard on her?"

"Not even a little, but I think you were honest. Anybody who works in law enforcement in any detail has to be prepared to be exposed to dangerous situations from time to time. Ariel is a sweet young woman, but she's not a child. You have to be straight with her, or it could end up hurting all of us."

Winter nodded, his words reflecting the same thoughts in her brain. Funny how often he managed to do that. "I think I need a few days off too. Maybe I should close the office, and we could take that vacation you keep going on about."

His eyes narrowed playfully. "Don't play with me now, darlin'."

"I wouldn't dare."

Her phone started to ring where it sat on the table between them. Winter set down her coffee and looked at the display, thinking it might be Davenport looking for more details on everything that had gone down yesterday.

Suzannah Hall-Tolle.

A sigh emanated from the deepest recesses of Winter's lungs. This was why she'd put it on silent all night. With great reluctance, she answered. "This is Winter."

"Finally!" the woman cried, her voice hurried and breathy. "I've been trying to get ahold of you all morning."

"I have an injury. I was sleeping in." Winter had clicked the phone to *Ringer* but hadn't even checked her messages yet.

"An injury. What kind of injury? Are you all right to work?"

Winter brushed a hand through her hair. "I'll be out of the office for a few days, but—"

"Well, that's hardly surprising."

"Excuse me?"

"I must say, I've been disappointed by your lack of investment." Suzannah's tone bit into Winter's ear. "I thought you of all people would understand the urgency of my nephew's situation."

"I'm sorry, but I do have other cases—"

"And how many of those involve young boys whose lives were entirely destroyed by your brother's actions?"

Winter cringed and clenched her teeth tight. She had a sudden urge to punch something.

"You left me with no choice," Suzannah continued, "but to hire another P.I. to assist with the investigation. I sent him around to Guy's place the day before yesterday and had him install surveillance cameras all over the property."

"You realize that's very illegal."

Noah leaned in. "Who are you talking to?"

She held a finger to him and mouthed, *I'll tell you in a minute*.

"I told you before, I'm willing to do whatever's necessary to protect my nephew. In fact, I've collected some damning footage of Guy's ineptitude already. I've sent it to your email for review."

"I really do not appreciate you going behind my back and hiring someone else to do your dirty work…and then sending me tainted evidence."

"As I said, you left me no choice."

Winter's hand balled into a fist, but that hurt her shoulder, so she loosened it. "Even if the footage is as damming as you say, it was obtained illegally, which means it's inadmissible in court."

"So?"

"So you said your goal was to get legal custody of Timothy."

"Timothy?" Noah looked alarmed, even a bit disappointed.

Winter turned away from him. "Spying on Guy is not going to help you do that. In fact, you might've just ruined your chances."

"You're supposed to be on my side!" The woman's voice was shaking and shrill. "I can't believe you. Don't you care that the boy is being abused?"

Winter took a deep breath. The nightmares she'd been having about Timothy swelled in her head, an amalgam of every dream smashed together into a single, stress-soaked whole. Then she thought about how she'd slept last night. Peaceful and easy, like everything was all right with the world.

Winter blinked and felt the warmth of tears on her eyelashes, a vague sparkle forming at the edges of her vision. "I'm sorry, Suzannah. I can't do this."

"Whatever do you mean?"

"I wish you nothing but luck, but I can't be involved in this anymore. Tim and I have too much history together. For both our sakes, I think it's better if I maintain distance between us. I honestly think it'd be for the best if Timothy and I never saw each other again."

"How can you say that? I thought you wanted to help. I thought you cared about him."

"I do care." Her voice choked with a sob. She quickly

wiped the tears from her eyes with her thumb. "I'm sorry, Suzannah. I really am. But please, don't contact me again."

Winter ended the call and dropped her phone on the table. Drawing her legs up close to her chest, she hugged them close and pressed her chin into her knee.

When Noah's hand brushed hers, she startled.

"I'm proud of you."

Winter grimaced. Then she closed her eyes and breathed out, trying to release the negative energy that had flooded her system.

Noah had been right. She had to leave Timothy in the past if she was going to keep her focus in the present. If she was going to have a future. She'd done everything she could for the boy. And as much as she was tempted to see him as more, he wasn't her family.

She had to let him go.

A cool breeze danced across Winter's face, drying the tears on her cheeks. She took Noah's hand in hers and squeezed it hard. He kissed her knuckles.

They sat in silence like that for a long time and watched the cars go by. After a while, Noah picked up his own phone and started to scroll.

"There's a deal on tickets to Fiji right now…"

Winter laughed. She couldn't help herself. She felt like a ten-thousand-pound weight had been lifted from her shoulders. "I think we should go to a lake somewhere."

"A lake?" Noah grinned, charmingly befuddled.

"Yeah. I'm in the mood for a swim and to get out in nature." Winter smacked her lips, realizing how badly she needed to brush her teeth. "When is my dang rock climbing stuff gonna show up?"

"You are not climbing any mountains with your shoulder like that."

"Duh. That's why I said lake."

"Hmm." Noah stroked his chin in thought. "It's still gonna be cold as hell this time of year."

"Whatever. I think it'd feel good after all the heat I've been under."

"All right. You're on." He rose from his seat, his smile growing. "We could always head out to Lake Pflugerville."

Winter giggled. "Gesundheit."

"I heard Eve going on about it. She and her husband take her kids canoeing out there."

"Do you think we could rent a canoe?"

"Probably. Let me look it up."

"'Kay. I'm gonna go pack up a picnic. This is going to be great!" She kissed his cheek before whirling on her heel and starting toward the front door. She was pretty sure there was some turkey and pesto in the fridge. She might not have been much of a cook, but she knew how to make a good sandwich.

As Winter drew open the screen, she paused at the sight of a yellow cab pulling up in front of their house. The door opened, and a black duffel bag was tossed onto the curb.

Winter put a hand up to shield her eyes as a tall man with gray hair and a big bald spot on top climbed out.

His gray eyes met hers, and a big smile broke across her face.

"Kline?" Winter set down her coffee cup and tied up her robe as she rushed down the porch toward him.

"Winter." He smiled weakly as he picked up his duffel and took a few slow steps closer.

When she reached his side, she wasn't quite sure what to do. Part of her wanted to hug him. Another part of her felt like even a handshake might be too intimate. But no amount of awkwardness could change just how happy she was to see the biological father who'd appeared so abruptly in her life and then left without so much as a goodbye.

She'd been worried—in a subconscious way she didn't

want to fully acknowledge—that she was never going to see him again. A second weight lifted from her shoulders, and she felt like she could float away.

She put out her hand, and Kline clasped it tightly with both of his, a kind of almost hug.

It was everything she needed.

"I'm sorry I left you in the lurch. I'm not used to people caring when I come and go."

"No worries," she lied, before following it up with the truth. "I'm really happy to see you."

Noah jogged down the steps to her side and set his heavy hand on her uninjured shoulder. Then he extended a hand to shake. "Kline."

"Noah." They shook.

"I'm so sorry about Opal." Winter blurted it out, thinking of the aunt she'd never meet. "Have there been any developments in the case?"

"Yes. We need to talk."

Noah took Kline's bag from him and threw it over his boxy shoulder. "Come inside. Are you hungry? I could reheat you some breakfast."

"Thank you." Kline nodded, but the expression on his face was strange. His lips were pursed to one side, eyes wandering.

Noah headed for the house at a brisk pace, leaving Winter and Kline to themselves.

They went up on the porch and sat down in the same chairs she and Noah had occupied a moment before.

As Winter watched his face, a chill was growing in her chest. "What's going on?"

Kline sat perched on the edge of the chair, almost as if he was ready to take flight again at any moment. "The cops released me, obviously. I didn't have a good alibi, but they found some evidence pointing elsewhere."

She furrowed her brow. "What evidence?"

"I've found out more about Opal and how she died. I mean, why she died." Kline forced the air from his lungs, then finally met her gaze. There was an emptiness inside them, a darkness.

Fear.

Winter's mouth went dry. She swallowed hard. "What is it?"

"Brace yourself." His blue eyes searched her face. "You're really not going to like it."

The End
To be continued...

Thank you for reading.
All of the Winter Black Series books can be found on Amazon.

ACKNOWLEDGMENTS

The past few years have been a whirlwind of change, both personally and professionally, and I find myself at a loss for the right words to express my profound gratitude to those who have supported me on this remarkable journey. Yet, I am compelled to try.

To my sons, whose unwavering support has been my bedrock, granting me the time and energy to transform my darkest thoughts into words on paper. Your steadfast belief in me has never faltered, and watching each of you grow, welcoming the wonderful daughters you've brought into our family, has been a source of immense pride and joy.

Embarking on the dual role of both author and publisher has been an exhilarating, albeit challenging, adventure. Transitioning from the solitude of writing to the dynamic world of publishing has opened new horizons for me, and I'm deeply grateful for the opportunity to share my work directly with you, the readers.

I extend my heartfelt thanks to the entire team at Mary Stone Publishing, the same dedicated group who first recognized my potential as an indie author years ago. Your collective efforts, from the editors whose skillful hands have polished my words to the designers, marketers, and support staff who breathe life into these books, have been instrumental in resonating deeply with our readers. Each of you plays a crucial role in this journey, not only nurturing my growth but also ensuring that every story reaches its full potential. Your dedication, creativity, and finesse have been nothing short of invaluable.

However, my deepest gratitude is reserved for you, my beloved readers. You ventured off the beaten path of traditional publishing to embrace my work, investing your most precious asset—your time. It is my sincerest hope that this book has enriched that time, leaving you with memories that linger long after the last page is turned.

With all my love and heartfelt appreciation,
Mary

ABOUT THE AUTHOR

Nestled in the serene Blue Ridge Mountains of East Tennessee, Mary Stone crafts her stories surrounded by the natural beauty that inspires her. What was once a home filled with the lively energy of her sons has now become a peaceful writer's retreat, shared with cherished pets and the vivid characters of her imagination.

As her sons grew and welcomed wonderful daughters-in-law into the family, Mary's life entered a quieter phase, rich with opportunities for deep creative focus. In this tranquil environment, she weaves tales of courage, resilience, and intrigue, each story a testament to her evolving journey as a writer.

From childhood fears of shadowy figures under the bed to a profound understanding of humanity's real-life villains, Mary's style has been shaped by the realization that the most complex antagonists often hide in plain sight. Her writing is characterized by strong, multifaceted heroines who defy traditional roles, standing as equals among their peers in a world of suspense and danger.

Mary's career has blossomed from being a solitary author to establishing her own publishing house—a significant milestone that marks her growth in the literary world. This expansion is not just a personal achievement but a reflection of her commitment to bring thrilling and thought-provoking stories to a wider audience. As an author and publisher, Mary continues to challenge the conventions of the thriller genre, inviting readers into gripping tales filled with serial killers, astute FBI agents, and intrepid heroines who confront peril with unflinching bravery.

Each new story from Mary's pen—or her publishing house—is a pledge to captivate, thrill, and inspire, continuing the legacy of the imaginative little girl who once found wonder and mystery in the shadows.

Discover more about Mary Stone on her website.
www.authormarystone.com

- facebook.com/authormarystone
- x.com/MaryStoneAuthor
- goodreads.com/AuthorMaryStone
- bookbub.com/profile/3378576590
- pinterest.com/MaryStoneAuthor
- instagram.com/marystoneauthor

Printed in Great Britain
by Amazon